ALSO BY MICHAEL NEWTON

GIDEON THORN

Skinwalker

Leviathan Rising

GHOST TOWN

GHOST TOWN

GIDEON THORN
BOOK 3

MICHAEL NEWTON

GHOST TOWN

PROLOGUE

LAZARUS, KANSAS: SEPTEMBER 25, 1864

"It's gettin' on toward midnight," Archie Clement said.

"Be's good a time as any," answered William Anderson, known to his enemies and certain of his friends as "Bloody Bill."

Anderson's fifty men were lined up in two mounted columns, ready to proceed. While Johnny Rebels in their hearts and to the marrow of their bones, they dressed in Union blue they'd stolen from a troop train in Missouri, getting ready for the raid Bill led tonight.

It wouldn't be the first time that guerrillas from Missouri crossed the state line into "Bleeding Kansas" to harass the Wheat State's abolitionists. The slaughter had begun in 1855, with some of it repaid in kind by free-soil killers led by John Brown and his sons before they went too far and wound up paying with their lives for the attack on Harper's Ferry. Advocates of slavery had sacked the town of Lawrence back in 1856, and while Missouri failed to join the rest of Dixie in seceding from the Union five years later, raiding still went on, by the Confederate irregulars loyal to Anderson and sometime ally William Quantrill. A combined force under Anderson and Quantrill hit Lawrence a second time in April 1863, seeking a band of Kansas "Redlegs" who had terrorized Missouri earlier, but they had only managed to assassinate 180-odd civilians after burning down a quarter of the town.

Anderson had personally gunned down fourteen men in Lawrence, and he wanted to improve that score tonight, in Lazarus.

The town's crime was permitting members of the Ninth Cavalry Regiment to pitch their tents outside of Lazarus and operate from there against what abolitionists called "Border Ruffians" devoted to the cause of slavery. Although a Kansas regiment, the Ninth had crossed the line into Missouri on occasion, where its men had killed a few Rebels and roughly handled certain women. While preparing for the raid, Bill's men had raided Huntsville's downtown business district, killing one man Anderson wrongly suspected was a U.S. marshal, stealing forty thousand dollars from the town's depository. The *St. Joseph Herald* branded Bloody Bill "the Devil," and he seemed to glory in it.

If he had his way, he'd earn that label for all time tonight, in Lazarus.

With men like Archie Clements, brothers Frank and Jesse James, and others of their ilk behind him, Anderson believed that he was on the verge of making history.

"Move out," he ordered Clements.

Archie passed the order on, then put his mount in step with Bill's as they moved toward the small town's scattered lights, two ranks of twenty-four men each riding behind them, each man carrying at least one long gun and a minimum of half a dozen pistols, to save time on reloading once the battle had been joined. For close-up work, they carried cutthroat razors, Bowie knives, and Arkansas toothpicks, all honed down to the limit for a killing slice.

One skinny kid in blue was standing guard, after a fashion, over the Ninth Regiment's campsite as Bloody Bill approached it, east of town. The lookout saw them coming in the light shed by a pale third quarter moon and moved to intercept them as he had been trained, despite their uniforms that matched his own. It was a ritual to be observed in war and peacetime, as a matter of routine.

"Halt!" he cried out, his Springfield rifle musket held port arms, ready for inspection or to raise and fire at need, depending on the situation that confronted him. "Who goes there?"

"Merrill's Horse," Anderson lied, then clarified it for the guard who still looked wet behind the ears. "Second Missouri Cavalry."

Seeing the gleam of captain's bars on Anderson's collar, the lookout dared to ask, "What brings you here, sir?"

"Some unfinished business," Anderson replied, and shot the youngster in the face with one of his four Colt Dragoon Revolvers, blowing out the kid's left eye and dropping him stone dead before he knew what hit him.

Bill's shot got the party started, his guerillas charging forward, whooping Rebel yells as they rode in among the Ninth Regiment's tents, firing through canvas at the sleeping forms within. According to Bill's field intelligence, no more than thirty-five troopers were camped outside of Lazarus, and few of those managed to rise before the hail of bullets finished them, no more than five emerging from their tents in underwear, with weapons in their hands, to die like soldiers fighting out of uniform.

From there, the town lay open, undefended. Anderson

saw lamplight shining out of certain windows now, the first, brisk storm of gunfire having wakened the civilian residents. Some of them would undoubtedly be armed, and while a handful might have joined in raids against pro-slavers in the past, none of them had been trained to fight the kind of men who followed Bloody Bill.

To say the slaughter went as planned can only soften its impact, downplay its individual atrocities. In the initial charge, Bill's raiders leaped down from their horses, bursting into shops and homes along the town's one street, with screams and gunshots echoing their entry. Citizens of Lazarus who tried to fight were shot down on the spot, or knifed to death if it was more convenient and pleasurable for the rampaging guer-rillas. Women of a certain look were stripped and raped repeat-edly before a bullet or a flashing blade ended their suffering. Each building that the raiders left was soon engulfed in flames.

The massacre did not proceed entirely within shops and homes, however. Roughly half the population, still in night-clothes or in none, was herded from their dwellings at gunpoint and forced to run a gauntlet of the Rebels, weeping as they hobbled toward a church that reared its steeple on the western edge of town. Bill Anderson himself kicked in the chapel's doors and watched, smiling, as his men drove the captives in.

So far, he'd killed five men with his own hand in Lazarus, and he was far from finished yet.

Inside the church, while Rebs disguised as Yanks crowded more than a hundred men, women, and children toward the altar, the town's minister stood at his pulpit, hands raised overhead and crying out for those under the gun to calm themselves and cease their wailing.

"God protects us!" he declared, hair wild around his

long and weathered face. "Remember that he loves us most in our extremity! Sing with me now, brothers and sisters, 'Leaning on the Everlasting Arms'!"

He began alone, most of his congregation still in tears, singing a soulful baritone.

"What a fellowship, what a joy divine,

"Leaning on the everlasting arms;

"What a blessedness, what a peace is mine,

"Leaning on the everlasting arms."

By the time he got to the refrain, roughly one-quarter of the prisoners joined in with feeble voices.

"Leaning, leaning, safe and secure from all alarms;

"Leaning, leaning, leaning on the everlasting arms."

Bill Anderson stood marveling, caught up in the discordant hymn, before he shouted to his men, "Join in, you bastards! Sing 'em home!"

Doubtful at first, the raiders followed orders, pitching in with voices that were strained and hoarse from shouting in the street.

"O how sweet to walk in this pilgrim way,

Leaning on the everlasting arms;

O how bright the path grows from day to day,

Leaning on the everlasting arms."

Anderson's voice cracked as he bellowed, "Now send them on their way!" and raised a Colt Dragoon in each hand, fully loaded, pumping lead into the helpless choir.

A thunder of his men's guns followed, deafening inside the church, ending the hymn as the remaining citizens of Lazarus sang, *"I have blessed peace with my Lord so near."* A squall of Rebel bullets ripped through flesh and bone, exploding skulls, puncturing vital organs, drilling babies in their mothers' arms. The minister was screaming from his pulpit when a slug entered his open mouth and blew away the whole rear of his skull.

When all was silent and the last parishioner was dead, Anderson's men filed out, some of them with their eyes downcast, the brothers Frank and Jesse grinning with a few more of the bolder ones. Behind them, as the last man exited, Anderson closed the chapel doors and ordered no one in particular, "Fetch torches. Burn it down."

The church was blazing as the troop rode out of Lazarus, the cross atop its steeple limned in fire.

Anderson wondered whether he would see it in his dreams.

ONE

FORDYCE, MISSOURI: SEPTEMBER 16, 1875

The balding, one-eyed cannibal mounted the gallows steps
with hopping, awkward strides occasioned by his natural
deformity and by the shackles on his legs. Once he had
reached the top, flanked by a pair of deputies ready for
anything, he turned around to face the crowd, smiling with
crooked yellow teeth. The gapped incisors that remained
had been filed down to points like shark's teeth, honed for
rending manflesh.

Standing well back in the audience, Gideon Thorn
waited to find out what the lunatic would say. In point of
fact, it came down to the sneering recitation of a recipe for
beef stew substituting human flesh, and had the convict
cackling by the time he finished. On the platform at his
side, a local minister stood pale and silent, clinging to his
Bible with both hands. Some people in the crowd were
muttering, a couple of them jeering, while a number of the
ladies wept and one dropped swooning to the ground,
surrounded instantly by clucking caregivers.

From there, the hanging didn't take long, even though the cannibal—Roark Lindsay, said to be the last of his demented line—snapped at the deputy who snugged a hood over his head. The noose came next, while mumbled curses issued from inside the muslin bag, and then a sudden drop that broke the thirty-five-year-old man-eater's neck.

Thorn left before they took the body down, bound for the livery to make his exit without fanfare from Fordyce and Bates County, bound for Kansas to the west. His work was done here, and more mysteries awaited him, in the Sunflower State and far beyond.

Tracking the Lindsay clan, Thorn hadn't known at first that he was hunting humans. All the newspapers had told him was a tale of disappearances along the border, both sides of the line that separated Kansas from Missouri, but predominantly in the Show Me State or near enough that something could have crossed the boundary to feed. Scattered remains were few and far between, the evidence of gnawing on them totally ambiguous, suggesting either kills by unknown predators or scavenging by smaller animals after the missing folks were dead.

Some never surfaced, even in the smallest bits and pieces, but were simply gone.

Thorn had begun, as was his custom, talking to the locals—lawmen, politicians if they'd listen to him, but primarily the folks who lived in Fordyce and the territory that surrounded it. As usual, gossip purveyed no end of theories, ranging from mundane to the ridiculous—but Thorn ruled nothing out initially, lending an ear to one and all without disdain.

Over the course of nine long days, his personal suspicion focused on the Lindsays, known to neighbors as stand-offish, even in a region where most dwellers kept their noses strictly out of other people's business, sometimes under threat of death. Moonshiners cooked their whiskey in the wooded hollows of Bates County; smugglers trundled back and forth to Kansas, Oklahoma, even down to Arkansas with anything they thought might sell; and outlaws like the tough James-Younger gang still roamed at will, protected by their kinfolk from the Pinkertons.

But even in that secretive, soft-spoken world, the Lindsays ranked as *strange*.

For one thing, no one in the neighborhood recalled them ever marrying, yet children still cropped up from time to time, suspected to be products of inbreeding. None of them attended school, they only came to town on market days—one Saturday per month, if that—and they'd been known to fire potshots at trespassers without a posted warning on their property. Despite all that, Bates County's sheriff left the tribe alone, preferring to advise voting constituents to give the Lindsays ample room.

With all of that in mind, Thorn had surveilled the property for three nights running, hiding in the woods and risking God knew what if he was caught. On the third night —or the fourth morning, blurring into dawn—he'd seen three of the Lindsay men, all stooped over and waddling, bring a trussed-up woman to their farmhouse, struggling against her bonds and squealing through a filthy gag.

The toss-up in his mind was whether he should ride to fetch the sheriff back from Butler, ten miles distant, risking what might happen to the woman in his absence, or burst in and try to save her on his own. Barely a moment's thought propelled him toward the farmhouse, up across the porch, and through the sagging front door with his Winchester in hand.

He'd found the woman stripped down to her birthday suit and tied onto a homemade table, arms and legs splayed, while the family—four adult men, two women, and a child some four years old—clustered around the table, all of the adults brandishing knives or cleavers, ready for some butchering. Thorn barely registered a row of human limbs that dangled from a rafter near the black wood-burning stove before the Lindsays rushed him, more or less at once.

When the smoke cleared, three men and one of the women—sister to the men, as it turned out—were stone dead on the dirt floor of their hovel, Roark Lindsay and sister Sue Lynn shot, but still clinging to life. The child sat in a corner, mewling like a wolf cub taken from its parents by a trapper.

With the testimony of the near-miss victim Thorn had saved, one Madelyn Duchaine of Austin's Mill in Vernon County, Butler's judge had placed the Lindsay child in Gorman's Home for Orphaned Girls, sent the young woman Thorn had wounded with a rifle shot to Fulton's state hospital for the mentally deranged, and ordered Roark Lindsay to hang. It was a clean sweep, even if Thorn couldn't see his way clear to feel good about the clan's last two survivors.

Anyway, there would be no more victims, which was all police and politicians cared about.

And it was time for Thorn to go.

The sheriff reinforced it, telling Gideon, "You done us all a favor, I'll admit that. But if truth be told, I'd just as soon you didn't pass this way again."

Gideon had faced him squarely, saying, "I can't promise anything, but as it happens I have other work to do, elsewhere."

Leaving Missouri, he was bound for Breckenridge in Colorado, where more disappearances had been reported for the past nine months. That meant a 680-mile ride across Kansas to the Centennial State—admitted to the Union only six months earlier—where his earliest nightmares were rooted in the slaughter of his family when Thorn was two years old. Neither forgiven nor forgotten, those vague memories propelled him on his rootless wandering across the West, searching for answers that were always just beyond his reach.

Three weeks, at least, to cover that much ground. He would be camping out most of the time, happy to sleep under the stars unless the weather turned, and in that case he had a tent borne by his pack mule, Bell. Thorn was prepared for almost anything he might encounter on the trail or at his destination, though he still left ample room to be surprised.

The final truth, he figured—if and when he ever managed to discover it—would be the greatest shock of all.

And that was saying something, given what he'd seen already in his long trek west of the Big River.

Thorn left Fordyce as he had arrived, still little known or understood by any of its residents. A packed courtroom had listened to his testimony of his showdown with the Lindsays, but the prosecutor had not lingered on his reasons for arriving in the first place, following a trail of newspaper reports across four states. The fat, balding defense attorney hadn't bothered with his motives either, focused as he was upon the hopeless task of having Roark Lindsay declared insane, to join his sister in the state's lockup for lunatics.

Now he was leaving, mounted on the gray stallion he'd christened Shadow, trailed by Bell, carrying Thorn's essentials that would not fit in his saddlebags. A few townspeople idled on the hamlet's wooden sidewalks, watching as he passed out of their lives, but Thorn did not acknowledge them, expecting neither thanks nor commendation for what he had done.

It wasn't what he'd come for, strictly speaking, but if it relieved the small community of a persistent dread, then it was worth the risk and effort.

Next time, maybe he'd be closer to his goal.

Thorn's life had changed when he was still a toddler, witnessing the butchery that claimed his parents and his older brother in their simple home. He had survived the massacre with a reminder from the slayer, carved into his scalp on that November night and now a streak of white dividing his black hair between Thorn's forehead and his crown. He'd wound up in an orphanage, much like the Lindsay clan's youngest survivor, although not insane, but had been rescued from it by a servant of his last surviving relative, a maiden aunt in Boston with a mansion and a fortune to support it.

From the servant who'd been sent to fetch him—one Obi Magoro, born in Africa—Thorn would acquire the skills of native martial arts, using them first against the trust fund bullies who harassed him in the halls of Boston's Weatherford Academy, later applying them to sports and shining as an athlete, while his photographic memory ensured straight A's in academic courses. The combination of his grades and Aunt Drusilla's wealth had paved his way to Harvard University, where Gideon graduated *summa cum laude* in the Class of 1873. He was earmarked for Harvard's law school in the fall, but took that summer off to tour Europe as a breather from his studies in the halls of academia.

And while he was away, everything changed.

The news of Aunt Drusilla's sudden death had brought him home aboard the fastest steamship then available, although he missed her funeral. The reading of her will provided generously for Obi Magoro, now a trusted friend of Gideon's, and left the rest to her nephew, an adult at twenty-one.

Instead of going on to Harvard Law and looking for a place in one of Boston's august legal firms, Thorn had another plan. He'd never made peace with a lazy sheriff's verdict that a rogue grizzly or black bear wandering abroad and ravenous when all the others of its kind were hibernating in their caves had massacred his family. Granted, his memories of the event were fragmented and vague, but Gideon believed the answer must be *something else.*

He'd started with a visit to his old home site—no longer part of Kansas Territory since that sprawling entity had been divided to create neighboring Colorado at the end of February 1861—but found his parents' cabin long since leveled, overgrown by crops, all traces of his infant tragedy erased. No old-timers remained to share their memories of the event, and so he had moved on, but with a purpose firm in mind.

To that end, Thorn pursued anomalies and unsolved mysteries throughout the West, tracking reports from newspapers and via word of mouth. Most of them wound up disappointing him, meaning they were resolved with mundane explanations: hoaxes, groundless rumors, fleeting glimpses of a well-known animal by persons unfamiliar with it, sometimes pure imagination run amok. There *had* been cases, though, where he was taken by surprise: a savage shapeshifter of sorts at Tularosa, in New Mexico, and a bizarre flying monstrosity in Arizona Territory among others, that had taxed Thorn to the limit, nearly adding him to their lists of the mutilated dead.

His hope was that someday, somewhere, one of the endless puzzles might shed light on what had happened to his family, however indirectly, handing Gideon a clue that he could work with as he labored to resolve the haunting riddle of his childhood. Until then, he roamed the length and breadth of half the continent, alone but for his animals, occasionally touching base by telegraph with old friend Obi or the team of lawyers and accountants pledged to manage Aunt Drusilla's large estate.

Thorn was a hunter tracking unknown prey in unfamiliar territory, but it suited him. Aside from his small arsenal of weapons and his photographic memory, he was well suited to the task in other ways. Completely ambidextrous with either pen or pistol, he was never easily surprised. From childhood, furthermore, he'd honed an innate gift for silent animal communication via thought alone, a trait he did not fully understand or share with others of his own species. Contact with animals depended partly on their stage of evolution: mammals were the easiest, then certain birds, on down the scale to reptiles and amphibians, then on to fish. He had no luck with insects but respected them and let them live in peace unless they threatened him somehow and there was no way out except employing force.

Peculiar, certainly, by "normal" human standards and

best not discussed. Sometimes, when he was in a pensive mood or on the verge of sleep, Gideon wondered whether it had anything to do with his escape from sudden death when he was two years old, bearing the mark of contact with his family's assassin. So far, there was no answer to that which any ardent introspection could reveal.

Thorn's quest was perilous, of course. Besides the Tularosa skinwalker and Arizona's flying dragon that had tried to eat him, humans sometimes took offense at his intrusion on their local mysteries. Lawmen, like the Bates County sheriff who had cautioned him against returning, often harbored jealousy about their jurisdiction, even—or particularly—when they'd failed to solve a string of grisly crimes. Many civilians also shared that take on Thorn's peculiar avocation, balking when he tried to question them about lost loved ones or seek help in running down a lead.

A few had tried to end his search by killing him, most recently the Lindsays in Bates County, but his hands were swift, his aim steady enough to put them down. It wasn't something Thorn enjoyed by any means, but neither did it spoil his sleep at night.

The press, meanwhile, could be his friend or enemy. While Thorn relied on newspaper reports for tips on many of his cases, small-town editors alert for "scoops" regarded him with curiosity, seeking a chance to rake over his history and pick his brain. While Gideon often cooperated to a point, hoping that a strategic article or two might smooth the way for him with locals in the know, he had been burned on several occasions by reporters who believed themselves adept at mind-reading, attributing a range of outré motives to his endless search, painting him as a upstart meddler, hapless Don Quixote, or a money-grubbing fraud.

They had been wrong on all counts, some deliberately so. Thorn's history—at least in his view—had entitled him to delve the West's strange mysteries, and he had never yet mistaken any farmer's windmill for a monster. As for money, he had plenty of his own, accepting no more than a free meal on occasion when his intervention solved a riddle or forestalled a brutal crime.

If forced to guess, Thorn might have said as many of his casual acquaintances in towns he'd visited regarded him with friendship as with doubt or scorn—but how did that make any difference? He wasn't seeking office or competing in a popularity contest. The quest was *his,* for him alone, and for the memory of his dead family.

And would he ever solve that mystery?

On days and nights like those after he left Missouri, riding on his own or camping under moon and stars in Kansas, Gideon had no idea. He might go on forever—well, until he died, at least—and never learn a thing about his parents' or his brother's fate. And after death, if anything existed on the "Other Side," it might still be a cruel, insoluble enigma like the limit of the universe or the "secret" of life.

But he would *try*, damn it. He'd do his best along the road that stretched before him, taking mental notes and trying to arrange the puzzle pieces into something he could recognize.

And when he saw it—*if* he saw it—what change would it wreak on him?

That was beyond Thorn's contemplation. Even though he wore a necklace bearing symbols of the world's major religions—Judaism, Christianity, Islam, and paganism—none of them answered the questions nearest to his heart. He didn't pray for guidance on his quest, convinced that there must be too many gods or none at all to bother with his personal concerns.

The road stretched out in front of him, its next stop Breckenridge. And after that...?

Another mystery on hold until tomorrow or some other day, always assuming that he lived that long.

TWO

Delbert Akins, long accustomed to the rocking of a stagecoach as he traveled far and wide, sat back and tried to sleep, a well-worn bowler hat pulled low over his eyes. He was aware of other passengers around him, five in all, that made the coach feel claustrophobic even with the windows gaping and the canvas flaps that served as covers for them during rain and dust storms rolled up tight and tied with leather thongs. Four horses drew the stage and kept it jolting on the unpaved track that residents of southern Kansas called a road.

Akins was in a window seat, left side and facing forward, slumped against the bulkhead of the coach as he focused on dozing off. The other passengers, all briefly introduced on boarding, had been seated in the coach first come, first served. None of them interested Akins in the least, but he was conscious of their presence, felt some of them watching as he tried to sleep.

Directly to his right sat Orin Pinkham, heavyset, red-faced from sun, drink, high blood pressure, or a combination of all three. He wore a derby similar to Akins's, but gray instead of black, and he was balding underneath it, compensating with a thick mustache. His stomach strained the vest of his gray three-piece suit, custom-tailored once upon a time but not too recently. If Akins had to guess, he would have said that Pinkham was between jobs at the moment, maybe on his way to some fresh start and dreading it.

To Pinkham's right and filling the front-facing seat was their star passenger, Julius Coffey, recently elected to the Kansas House of Representatives, replacing an incumbent from Chautauqua County who had died within a week of his selection by that county's voters, two months earlier. A relatively young man, well coiffed, with a short, neat beard, he seemed to charm the ladies but his looks were lost on Akins and the other men on board.

Those ladies sat across from Akins, facing toward the rear. Directly opposite was Laurel Dycus, introduced to her companions as a governess en route to join a family in Hays City, whose father worked in banking while the mother did her best to cope with three young children. In her thirties, auburn hair pinned up beneath a feathered lady's touring hat. Akins had made note of her figure but could not have said how much was helped along by a determined corset underneath her clothes.

Next to the governess sat Florence Mottinger, and to her left, her husband Eldridge, proud to say he was an agent for the U.S. Bureau of Indian Affairs, en route from his former post in Indian Territory to South Dakota's Crow Creek Reservation, housing Sioux removed from Minnesota after the Dakota War of 1862. He called it a promotion, but his wife—a stiff sort, pinched of face—was visibly unhappy with the change.

Nothing to me, thought Akins, who had earned his living with a deck of cards since he was seventeen years old. And thinking that, he drifted off to sleep.

Lucky bastard, thought Laurel Dycus. Wish that I could sleep like that aboard this rattletrap.

It was not how a proper governess should think, much less a sentiment she would express aloud, but as it happened, Laurel was not a governess and never been one. That was her cover story, dodging questions that she didn't want to answer where her background was concerned. She'd worked in brothels from New Jersey to Missouri in her time, starting at sixteen years of age, using her skills to build a clientele and rising to a madam's rank at twenty-eight. After three years in Springfield she was moving west again, with no determined destination, thinking vaguely of Topeka, maybe Denver, or a turn in California if her cash held out.

The trouble back in Springfield stemmed from one of Laurel's girls who's slashed a businessman and left him scarred for life. Granted, the drunken prick had beaten her as if she were his dog at home, unmindful of the cutthroat razor in her nightstand. Self-defense was not acceptable to Springfield's marshal, though, particularly after certain socialites accused him of accepting cash and other favors to permit the brothel's operation within sight of Greene County's courthouse. Someone had to go, and since the marshal had a badge and gun, Laurel Dycus was the sacrificial goat.

Now she was starting fresh, three thousand dollars in her handbag, with a .22-caliber Colt Open Top Pocket Model Revolver and a folding knife from France, one of their pearl-handled *Châtellerault* switchblades that opened at the touch of a brass button. No razors for the madam; if she had to cut a rowdy customer she would be doing it in style.

Her fellow passengers aboard the coach would have been shocked, perhaps outraged, to hear the truth of Laurel's history. She recognized them as the sort who posed as straitlaced moralists in public, during daylight hours, then turned out to rent a woman for a bit of fun after the sun went down. All but the man who sat across from her, that is. She would have known Del Akins as a gambler even if he hadn't been so frank about it when the lot of them were introduced in Springfield, loading up the coach.

And Mrs. Mottinger was also a familiar type. Given a chance, she'd join the Ladies' League or its equivalent and prattle about cleaning up whatever town she lived in, running out the whores, gamblers, saloonkeepers and such. She might have known her husband was a patron of the people she despised, or maybe she concealed that knowledge from herself behind a screen of moral piety. If Florence Mottinger had ever had a day—or night—of true joy in her life, she'd managed to disguise it with a vague expression of contempt that seemed to be perpetual.

And it was wives like that, as Laurel knew, who drove their husbands off to bars and brothels where they sought a bit of peace from strife and storm.

Eldridge Mottinger, though bland of visage with his fellow travelers, was gloomy when he thought about his prospects at the Crow Creek Reservation. At his last post, with the Choctaw Nation, he had been in charge, a veritable god over the tribesmen who had foolishly supported the Confederacy in the Civil War and got their just desserts by being driven from their Mississippi homelands into the relative wasteland of Indian Territory. Mottinger had ruled them as a stern but benevolent tyrant—by his lights, at least—and suppressed any tremors of red man's resentment by force.

He had been riding high, and earmarked for an office job in Washington, D.C., when paperwork betrayed him. Afterward, disgraced, Mottinger struggled to explain that simple errors in his bookkeeping had misplaced several thousand head of cattle slated for the reservation and he had no clear idea of where they'd gone, despite persistent rumors that white ranchers had acquired them at a premium. Likewise, when auditors sent from the nation's capital found careless mathematical mistakes in Mottinger's financial ledgers, he had pleaded ignorance. A Secret Service agent came to ask him where the money was, but it was never found.

And if Mottinger had his way, it never would be.

There'd been talk of charges being filed, some whispered mentions of embezzlement, but in the end, while Mottinger claimed innocence and railed against his enemies for slander, no hard evidence against him could be found. And if the BIA could not indict him, neither did its leaders feel entitled to dismiss him outright. Rather, they'd consigned him to a kind of purgatory at Crow Creek, where Mottinger would work as an assistant to a man ten years his junior, until he finally got fed up and resigned.

Almost as bad as being transferred and demoted was the chill his wife put out whenever they were forced to share a common space. Never romantic, much less passionate, Florence was positively frigid toward him now, speaking only as bare necessity required—or, to ensure continued earnings from the government, when they were cast into official situations, banquets, and the like.

It was a drab, some might say ghastly way to live, but Eldridge Mottinger was used to it by now, approaching twenty years shackled to Florence as his ball and chain. Initially, he'd hoped to grab a piece of her affluent family's fortune, but her father's will had cut her out entirely as a married woman with a working husband, while her three brothers divided the estate valued at some three million dollars.

I should have divorced her then, he thought, not for the first time, but divorce was strictly frowned on by their church and by the federal establishment in Washington. Affairs were one thing, for a man, but breaking up a family could be the kiss of death in politics.

So it would be Crow Creek.

Mottinger closed his eyes and wondered what his new boss had been told about him, and if he would favor Mottinger with access to the reservation's books.

Orin Pinkham had secrets of his own. A former bank vice president from Kansas City, he had managed to embezzle some two hundred thousand dollars from the Rancher's Bank before his paranoia got the better of him, prompting nightmares and a string of daylight fantasies in which police were on to him, just waiting for a few more bits of evidence before they pounced. He'd started drinking heavily, saw it reflected in his work, and had been cashiered from the bank for "moral turpitude." Ironically, the president who had dismissed him didn't seem to know a thing about the missing cash, which Pinkham had accumulated as a hedge against some future rainy day.

And figuratively, it was pouring now.

He'd fled from Kansas City on a Sunday, traveling by train, then running out of tracks as he moved westward, settling for a seat aboard the creaky stage. No destination clear in mind, he'd spun the other passengers a tale about a job prospect waiting in Denver, but his true goal was a quiet place where he could dole his money out, live reasonably well, and manage to avoid arrest.

For all he knew, a warrant might be open on him now. The good news: he had left Missouri, so the law enforcement agents there were virtually powerless to haul him back for trial. Missouri's governor could try to extradite him, if some lawman ever tracked him down, but Pinkham worried more about the bounty hunters roaming far and wide over the West.

He'd studied this. Two years before, in *Taylor v. Taintor,* the U.S. Supreme Court had ruled that bounty hunters possessed powers far beyond those bestowed on sworn police and sheriffs. Men hunting a fugitive for money were allowed to cross state lines, break into homes or other buildings without warrants, seize the fugitive—kidnap him, in effect—and carry him back to whatever jurisdiction wanted him. If Rancher's Bank or someone else in Kansas City put a price on Pinkham's head, no place within the country offered sanctuary.

And the worst part was, he had no way to learn if such a bounty presently existed.

Alcohol soothed him some of the time, but only in increasing doses. He was desperate to find a hiding place, dig out a burrow for himself, and pull the dirt in after him.

Julius Coffey was the only passenger excited to be riding on the stage, as trying on the mind and body as it was. His predecessor's death had been a blessing for him, though he'd never speak those words aloud, coupled with the surprise of two rich merchants in Chautauqua County who regarded him as their personal voice in the state legislature, at Topeka. That was fine with Coffey, for the moment, just so long as they were paying him to vote as they preferred and kept the personal arrangement to themselves.

Unknown to those who'd bankrolled him, Coffey had plans that stretched beyond the Kansas House or Representatives or the state Senate. He already saw himself as governor, then U.S. Senator when he had built a name up for himself within the party as a man who understood both strength and compromise. Someday, after a proud career that made him rich and famous, he might even run for President of the United States.

Why not? The country was still young enough that relative nobodies sprung from humble roots could claw their way up to the top, wooing selected friends and jettisoning those who held them back. Consider Andrew Jackson, place of birth uncertain, educated in an "old-field school," apprenticed to a saddle-maker as a youth. Or Honest Abe Lincoln, born in a one-room Kentucky log cabin, educated for less than a year in total by wandering tutors, self-taught in law and rescued from the curse of anonymity by conflict over slavery.

Compared to those examples, Julius Coffey thought himself a paragon of ripe political potential. Already elected to substantial office at the age of twenty-five, he had the world laid out in front of him and sponsors paying him to seize it by the throat.

What young, ambitious man could ask for more?

"Whadda you think about this batch?" asked Dempsey Poppert, glancing at his shotgun guard before he snapped his reins and urged the four-horse team to greater speed.

"About like usual," said Warren Mapes, cradling his double-barreled coach gun in his lap. "Nobody stood out much to me."

"The governess ain't bad," Poppert allowed, shifting to make himself more comfortable on the cushion he had placed atop the driver's seat.

"Awright, I guess," Mapes granted. "But I seen better at Awful Annie's, back in Wichita."

"Them's sportin' ladies," said the driver.

"Sport was what I had in mind," the guard replied. "Ain't no use oglin' on the passengers."

Poppert knew he was right, but it was still a game the driver played, trying to guess whether the people he was carrying had told the truth about themselves when they were introduced to one another. No one told the *whole* truth, as he knew from longtime personal experience. Some who rode the stage were simple travelers, while others were in flight from one thing or another, making tracks before their troubles overtook them, dragged them down, and chewed them up like mongrels on a soup bone.

"Didn't care much for the other one," said Poppert. "Mrs. Mottinger, I mean."

"Dried-up old prune," Mapes said, like *he* was any kind of strapping youngster in his own right, pushing fifty-five years old with the arthritis starting in his hands. What he would do when they were too curled up to hold a shotgun, Poppert didn't care to think.

"I guess her husband likes her," he replied.

"Might do, might not," Mapes replied. "Could be for show. Says he's an Injun agent. Might have some papooses born the wrong side of the blanket."

"Well..."

"That politician now, he could be one to watch."

"Newly elected," Poppert said.

"I wonder who's promotin' him, down in Chautauqua."

"You don't think he got it on his looks?" the driver grinned.

"Not till they let the ladies vote in real elections, 'stead of just for school boards," Mapes opined. "And I don't see that happenin' until he's old and gray."

"You never know. They're gettin' organized."

"Stay home and organize the house is what I say. Who's watchin' all their kids while they parade around and wave their signs?"

Poppert, who'd never married and was now beyond it, didn't think about the cause of women's suffrage often, one way or the other. He preferred the sporting ladies too, who did what they were told and asked no questions, just so long as they were paid.

"I tell you, it'll be a strange damn world if women get to vote across the board," Mapes said. "Who's next? The redskins?"

"They ain't even citizens," said Poppert. "The Civil War

amendments only cover slaves. Make that *ex*-slaves. Injuns are sep'rate nations. You know that."

"Heard somethin' like it, but I didn't give a rip," said Mapes. "We haven't seen the last of trouble from 'em yet, no matter how many the government's got penned up on the reservations. You can take that to the bank."

"You're tellin' fortunes now?"

"I sniff the wind and know what's what," Mapes said.

"Might be a little clearer to you if you washed your clothes," said Poppert, chuckling.

"Look who's talkin'. When's the last time you sat in a bathtub, Dempsey?"

"Week ago last Thursday, if I recollect."

"You oughta check that calendar again," Mapes said. "Could be last year's."

"Now listen here—"

Coming around a curve, he reined in sharply, calling "Whoa!" out to the horses as he saw three riders sitting in the middle of the road. They all faced toward the coach and held long guns—two lever-actions and some kind of single-shot—braced on their hips, the muzzles pointed skyward. While the coach was slowing down, one of the men with a repeater, farthest off to Poppert's left, triggered a shot into the air.

"Stand and deliver!" he commanded in a ringing voice.

THREE

Thorn heard the rifle shot and pulled up short. Judging the volume of it, he decided it had come from roughly half a mile away, to the northwest of him. When there was no second shot, he pondered what it meant: a hunter on the prowl, maybe a cowboy startled by a snake—or was it something else entirely?

Something sinister?

The only way to settle that, Thorn realized, was to detour and have a look.

He passed the silent word to Shadow and the stallion instantly responded to a light tug on the reins, veering off course and trotting toward the gunshot's source. Bell, bringing up the rear, was less enthusiastic for the new direction and the change of pace but came along without an audible complaint.

One shot was difficult to pinpoint, some would say impossible, but if it was a sign of trouble Thorn expected he could track it down. The odds improved when he had covered some two hundred yards, meeting a road that ran across his former path from south to north. It wouldn't slow him down that much to ride along the road for half a mile or so, and if he came up empty-handed after that, he would resume his former course with nothing lost.

The missing persons he planned to investigate at Breckenridge were almost surely dead by now. They wouldn't notice if he took a few more minutes on the trail.

If there was trouble—and he wasn't taking it for granted yet—Thorn thought he was prepared for anything. He wore twin Colts, the Single Action Army models nick-named Peacemakers, and had a Winchester repeater cham-bered for the same .44-40 rounds, the lever-action Model 1873. For longer-distance work, he also packed an 1872 model Sharps rifle in .50-90 caliber, accurate to fifteen hundred yards with its custom-made, three-foot-long scope. If the action came to close quarters, a twelve-inch Bowie knife was sheathed on his gunbelt, and Thorn carried a smaller dagger on his right leg, with its grip protruding from his knee-high boot.

Ideally, there would be no shooting, much less killing, but he'd learned to take each situation as it came when he was in the wilderness and on his own. In cases where swift action was required, threatened by man or beast, Thorn would not hesitate.

The cannibals in Fordyce could have testified to that, if they were still alive.

The Kansas countryside was mostly flat, not cultivated land in this part of the state, scattered with trees that gave it the appearance of a chessboard in the middle of a game. The pawns were yuccas, while the larger pieces ran toward fir and cottonwood, elm, oak, and sycamore. The road, such as it was, wound past the varied clumps of trees and thereby shielded Thorn's approach to some extent, as he drew nearer to the shooting site.

And now he had to wonder, if there had been trouble, was he coming on the scene too late?

"First thing you gotta do," said Buford Muntz, "is toss that shotgun down. And you behind the reins, that Colt."

The stagecoach guard delayed reacting for a moment, glancing at his driver before he did anything. Muntz was about to drill him when the driver nodded, and the old man pitched his coach gun down onto the road, followed immediately by the driver's pistol. At the same moment, a man's head poked out of the forward-facing left-hand side and asked nobody in particular, "What's happening?"

"Shut up and stay inside till someone tells you diff'rent," Muntz replied. The head ducked backward, like a turtle's being drawn inside its shell.

On either side of Muntz, his pals—Laze Drenen to his right, Elmer Tutwiler to his left—sat waiting, silent, with their rifles angled toward the stagecoach now. They had it covered if the two men on the high seat made a move, or if the passengers tried bailing out on either side to cause a fuss.

Not that it mattered, since the bandits wore no masks and Muntz had never planned on leaving any witnesses alive.

"What are you carryin' today?" he asked the driver.

"Just passengers," the old man said. "Six of 'em, with their baggage."

Muntz frowned, hearing that. "No mail? No strongbox?" he demanded.

"Not this time. They run the mail on Mondays now, and this is—"

"Friday. Yeah, I know," Muntz interrupted him. "But what about the cash and such?"

"Wells Fargo mostly handles that, these days," the driver said.

Beside him, grinning to expose a gap in his front teeth, the guard opined, "Looks like you missed out all around, fellas."

"We ain't done yet," Muntz said. "Let's see them passengers and find out what they're carryin', then we can have a look inside their bags."

The driver's scrunched-up face told Muntz that he was thinking of a tart response, but the old man was smart enough to bite his tongue. Instead, he called out to the passengers, "Ladies and gents, kindly step out."

Ladies?

Muntz had to smile at that, but when the first woman stepped from the stage, getting a hand down from a portly fellow who was glaring at the holdup men, Muntz nearly grimaced. Saying she was in her forties might be generous, and the expression on her face could turn milk sour. She was skinny too, on top of that, despite the crinoline beneath her skirt.

The second female was a younger specimen, by ten or fifteen years, and well proportioned, carrying herself with what Muntz viewed as style. Her eyes were haughty, which he didn't mind, as long as she took orders when it counted and did nothing to infuriate him. As to what that might entail, it varied by the hour and the day.

The other passengers were men, ranging in age from thirty-something up to early fifties. All looked reasonably affluent, except the last one out, wearing a bowler hat and dark red vest that looked like it was made of satin. If that one wasn't a gambler, Muntz decided, he would eat his hat.

And what did that mean, for their score?

Some gamblers carried money with them for a stake in the next town, but just as many—maybe more—were broke when they left one place for another. His three male companions should have pocket money, watches, maybe something worth the taking in their luggage if his luck held out. The women should be good for jewelry, at least, and if they came up short the younger one could make him happy other ways, before he handed her to Tutwiler and Drenen.

Not a wasted stop entirely, but still disappointing if no secrets were revealed.

"Good morning, people," Muntz called out to them. "Today should be one you remember. Don't make it your last."

Del Akins had been robbed before. He knew the protocol and how to live through it, unless the bandits were already in a killing mood. As far as that went, it was still too early to be sure. He worked at staying calm, relaxing, thinking how he'd reach the derringer in his vest pocket if he needed it to stay alive.

Cash-wise, he had twenty-nine bucks and change, enough to get him started on a poker game in Great Bend, when he left the stage there. If he won, Akins had planned to stick around a while. Failing at that, he'd save enough to catch another stage or hop a westbound ride from there aboard the Atchison, Topeka and Santa Fe Railway. Now, it looked like he and all the others would be riding into Great Bend stony broke—if they arrived at all.

Some road agents, as Akins knew, preferred to leave no living witnesses behind. They used the scorched earth method, silencing whoever might betray them later in a court of law. If that turned out to be the case, there would be no convincing these three bandits that he wouldn't squeal. He simply would have drawn the wrong card and his fate was preordained.

If they already planned to kill him, Akins would not die without a fight. The derringer aside, he had a small dirk sheathed between his shoulder blades, suspended by a rawhide cord around his neck. Akins had used it half a dozen times before, once fatally, when he had been falsely accused of palming cards in Abilene and had to flee the city afterward, or face a necktie party.

In another situation, playing cards with some rough customers in Natchez, he'd been forced to use the derringer. No one had died that time, though one unruly drunk had lost an eye, and once again the law had shown Akins his walking papers, though without the shadow of a noose to hurry him along.

Long story short: he was a fighter when he had to be, and this could be another of those days.

Maybe the last one he would ever see.

Gideon Thorn was closer to the shooting scene than he'd expected when he saw the stagecoach standing still, four horses in its traces, half a dozen passengers on foot beside it and its two-man crew still huddled on the elevated driver's seat. Three mounted riflemen had stopped the coach, a robbery in progress, and were covering the hostages, their spokesman giving orders in a gravel voice.

"First thing," he said, "you men turn out your pockets, and you ladies dump your handbags. Laze will come around collectin' any cash or trinkets you might have, including watches and what have you in the way of jewelry. That's rings and earrings, bracelets, necklaces, no holdin' back if you all know what's good for you."

Thorn saw one of the riders step down from his brindle mare and leave its reins dangling as he advanced, doffing his hat to hold whatever he collected from the passengers. What kind of name was "Laze"? Thorn couldn't place it, but the part that bothered him was hearing it spoken aloud. The highwaymen weren't masked, and if they started tossing names around it made him think they planned on slaughtering the stage's passengers and crew.

What should he do?

Thorn was concealed within a stand of pawpaw trees beside the road, some fifty yards behind the coach. He could start shooting, ruling out the single-shot scoped Sharps in favor of his Winchester, but that would jeopardize the holdup's victims when the highwaymen replied in kind. A clean sweep meant he had to drop one of them, preferably two, and catch whoever still remained before they had a chance to fire.

Unlikely, but it could be done.

He eased the lever-action rifle from its saddle boot, dismounted, and dispatched a silent calming message to his animals. Both were inured to gunfire, Shadow more or less a war horse in his own right, but Thorn moved away from them regardless, edging through the trees until he'd closed the gap a little more.

He didn't have to prime the Winchester, since Thorn kept a live cartridge in its chamber for emergencies. There'd be no *click-clack* racket to betray him when he simply thumbed the hammer back and aimed to fire. The question now was whether he should kill from ambush in cold blood or try something a little fancier to get the drop on the three stick-up men and force them to disarm.

Thorn never pulled a trigger lightly, wouldn't kill if he could possibly avoid it, but in situations such as this one, the eight victims had to be his first priority.

Drawing a deep breath and releasing part of it, he held the rest and sighted down his weapon's barrel toward his chosen target.

Dempsey Poppert had been driving teams for over twenty years. He'd driven mule teams, ore wagons and Conestogas, shifting over to the Barlow & Sanderson Company in 1869 and piloting their coaches ever since. No stranger to the risks involved, he'd shot it out with bandits once before, nobody hit on either side, but now he was unarmed aside from a small pocketknife he couldn't reach.

The one called Laze was ambling toward the passengers, hat held in front of him like a collection plate in church. He had a rolling kind of walk, reminding Poppert of a sailor stranded on dry land, and smiled too much for someone who had all his faculties. The Henry rifle that he carried was an old one, but the shooter still could drop most anything he aimed at with it. Figure sixteen shots in that one, and another fifteen in the leader's Winchester, before the third man had to use his Maynard .52-caliber carbine.

"We're done," he cautioned his companion on the high seat, whispering.

"How's that?" Mapes challenged him, too loudly.

"Hush!" he hissed. "They got no masks, and now we know one of 'em's name."

"So what?" Mapes whispered back, then got his meaning. "Ah, hell no."

"And we already threw our guns away."

"Clam it, you two!" the outlaw leader barked at Poppert. And in case he'd missed the point, added, "Just keep your goddamn pie holes shut."

"Yessir," the driver answered back, pushing his luck.

When he had joined Barlow & Sanderson there was an oath involved, something about defending passengers and cargo with his life. Poppert had never taken that too seriously until now, when it seemed clear to him that the holdup men planned on a one-way shooting match no matter how much they collected from the coach. And since it looked like he was bound to die...

The leap down from the driver's seat was ten feet, easily, requiring steps to climb aboard. It would take nerve to fling himself headlong on top of an armed man, but in the circumstances, what choice did he have? The sole alternative was sitting like a target in a shooting gallery and letting someone pick him off without a fight.

No thanks.

One thing that Dempsey Poppert still had going for him was his scrappiness. He'd never run from trouble in his life and didn't plan on starting now, down at the end of it. He had no family to think about how he'd gone out, but damn it, every man had pride.

Maybe, before he jumped, he'd have a chance to reach that pocketknife.

Thorn scanned the scene one final time, made his last-second calculations, and decided that he didn't have to kill with his first shot. What happened after that would be the bandits' choice.

The mouthpiece for the trio was their leader, obviously. When Thorn made his move, the dumpy looking fellow with the Winchester would call the tune for all that followed, whether his companions dropped their guns or opened fire and turned the situation from a holdup to a bloodbath. Either way, Thorn knew he could not safely let the robbery proceed.

Murder or worse was waiting at its end.

He lined up on the leader's rifle, braced across the saddle horn on his classic overo stallion, angled toward the coach somewhere between the two men on their high seat and the passengers huddled below. When he squeezed off, the *crack* of his Winchester froze the small tableau behind a haze of smoke.

Thorn's bullet struck the wooden foregrip of the bandit leader's rifle, shattered it, and tore the weapon from his hand. The buttstock slammed into his target's ribs at the same time and nearly spilled the outlaw from his saddle, but he clutched the horn with his left hand in time to save himself from falling.

And before the others could react, Thorn pumped the lever-action on his rifle, calling out to them, "Don't move! You're covered!"

Number one was cursing fluently, shaking his bruised right hand, but he managed to tell his two comrades, "Hold up boys!" Then he shouted toward the trees where Thorn's gunsmoke still hovered in the air, "The hell are you? Whadda you want?"

"First thing," Thorn said, "all three of you throw down your weapons. That means all of them, from rifles down to knives. One funny move from anyone, you all go down."

It wasn't quite a bluff, though harder to pull off than Thorn had made it sound. The two still packing long guns turned eyes toward their leader, who delayed a moment, then commanded them, "Do like he says."

A rain of steel dropped to the ground: two rifles, four revolvers, and three hunting knives. The red-faced bandits glared around, from Thorn's semi-concealed position in the pawpaw grove, back to the travelers they'd been intent on robbing. Thorn allowed some movement to his Winchester, not framing any single target in his sights, ready to fire wherever there was need if someone made a foolish move.

"Next thing," he said, "the two still mounted get down from your animals. Bring all three back behind the coach and tie their reins up to the rear boot."

Grudgingly, with dead-eyed glares and muttered curses, the marauders did as they were told. While they were at it and he had them covered, Thorn addressed the stagecoach passengers and crew. "Round up their weapons now. A couple of you gents keep those three covered, while the rest put their remaining hardware in the coach."

Without delay, the driver and his erstwhile guard climbed down to claim their guns, aiming a Colt and double-barreled coach gun at the outlaws while their passengers retrieved the other weapons, piling them inside the footwell of the stage. When that was done, the unarmed bandits under guard, Thorn led Shadow and Bell out of the pawpaw grove and into view, his Winchester leveled one-handed at the fuming bandits.

"We can do this one of two ways," he told everyone. "First is to leave these three on foot and drop their mounts a few miles north to graze, in case they want to fetch them."

"But they'll get away with this atrocity!" the older of the female passengers protested.

"Yes they will, and have to start from scratch to pull another job somewhere, I guess," Thorn granted. "The alternative would be to tether them beside their horses and proceed at walking pace until you reach the next town that can handle them. I don't know where that is or how long it would take."

That caused some muttering among the passengers, until the driver cut it off. "We're leavin' 'em," he said. "You folks get back on board. We're runnin' late." While the unhappy passengers were boarding, he asked Thorn, "You wanna ride with us a ways, young fella? I mean, just in case?"

Thorn thought about it for a moment, then replied, "I don't mind if I do."

FOUR

"A ways" turned out to be five miles by Thorn's rough calculation. He'd been following the stagecoach at his own pace, riding off to one side so he didn't have to eat their dust, and estimated passing time by placement of the sun above. He caught up when the coach slowed down, then stopped completely in the middle of the road.

By then, Thorn had already passed a sign proclaiming that a town called Lazarus was ten miles farther up the road. It rang a bell, somewhere in his subconscious, but he didn't care enough to think about it as he overtook the stage.

None of the passengers assisted when the driver and his shotgun guard climbed down to loose the outlaws' horses. Thorn stepped down from Shadow and pitched in as they untied the reins, then took the extra time required to strip the animals of tack, saddles, and blankets. The idea behind that thought was twofold, as the driver laid it out for Thorn while they were working: first, spare the three mounts from staying saddled, if their former riders never came to fetch them; second, slow the outlaws down another while if they *did* find the horses, putting all their riding gear back on.

When they were done, the driver—Dempsey Poppert, as he introduced himself, with Warren Mapes beside him—offered Thorn his thanks a second time. "You saved our bacon, son," he said. "There's no doubt in my mind them peckers meant to kill us men, and God knows what all with the ladies."

"Anybody would have done the same," Thorn said.

"Don't count on that," said Mapes. "You need to watch yourself in Kansas."

"That's a habit I developed early," Thorn replied.

"Okay, then," Poppert said. "We need to roll before them in the coach start grumblin'. Gotta make up time, you know."

"I'll likely head along this way a bit longer," said Thorn. "Maybe stop over for the night at Lazarus before I turn back west."

"We pass on through," the driver said. "Not likely that we'll meet again."

"Well, it's been interesting," Thorn replied.

He mounted Shadow, watched the driver and his side-kick climb aboard their high seat, while a couple of the passengers observed him from the coach's windows, their expressions curious. Thorn waited for the snap of reins and watched the stage roll out, gathering speed as it departed, plumes of dust rising from its big wheels. The outlaws' horses showed no agitation over being left behind, but rather turned to cropping grass along the roadside.

Urging Shadow forward, Thorn thought back to Lazarus and hit upon the reason it had twitched his memory. There'd been a massacre by Rebel cavalry—guerrillas if he had it right—during the Civil War, some years before the larger town of Lawrence—where he'd spent time in an orphanage before the war--was sacked by Quantrill's raiders. Thorn was vague on details, but he guessed survivors or new settlers had rebuilt the town to keep it going in peacetime.

Whatever, he could likely spend the night there, board his animals, and head west in the morning on his ride to Breckenridge. As for the stagecoach, it would be long gone by then, its meeting with the bandits nothing but an ugly memory.

Some memories, Thorn had discovered, faded over time, while others never went away. The latter kind might be unpleasant, or they might recall the finest moments of a person's life. In Thorn's case, they'd propelled him on a quest that seemed to have no end in sight. But he was working on it and could only forge ahead while life remained.

"So what 'n hell we doin' now?" Laze Drenen asked. "We's stuck on here, middle a nowhere."

"What we do is *walk*," said Buford Muntz. "Unless you'd rather sit down here and starve yourself to death."

"Walk *where?*" Elmer Tutwiler asked him, almost whining.

"Lemme think? How bout we go 'n find the horses?" Muntz replied.

"God knows how far they took 'em," Drenen said.

"Or if they'll even drop 'em off at all," Tutwiler added.

"Right, then. *I'll* go lookin' for the horses," Muntz growled at them. "You two wander off some other way and good luck to you. *Adios.*"

He hadn't walked but twenty feet or so before Muntz heard the others coming up behind him, grumbling. Just before they overtook him, Drenen said, "Wait up, will you? We're comin' too."

"Wait, nothin'," Muntz spat back. "You come with me, keep up, damn it!"

They'd covered half a mile or so, northbound through scrub brush following the road, when Drenen, sounding breathless, said, "We's gonna need more guns."

"Anybody ever take you for a genius?" Muntz inquired.

"Um, well..."

"He's playin' with you," Tutwiler advised.

"Oh, right. So what about the guns, Bu?"

"Horses first," Muntz said, saving his breath. "Guns later."

"Horses, right," Drenen agreed. "But once we get 'em— *if* we get 'em—then where do we go?"

"Where do you think?" Muntz asked.

"I wouldn't ask you if I knew, would I?"

"Awright. We go after the goddamn coach."

"The hell?" Tutwiler sounded as if he couldn't believe his ears.

"Where else?" Muntz challenged him. "Think about it. Number one, they got our guns, and number B, I don't take anybody's insult lyin' down. We meant to rob 'em and we's gonna, plus gettin' some righteous satisfaction for the way they treated us."

"That shooter dressed in black," Tutwiler said.

"I ain't forgettin' him," Muntz said.

How could he, when the sumbitch shot a rifle from his hands and likely ruined it, bruising his hand, forearm and ribs in the process? If Muntz had done the shooting, he'd have killed whoever he was aiming at and finished it right there. He didn't understand a man who missed on purpose, if it *was* on purpose, and he meant to teach the black-clad stranger that he'd made a serious mistake.

A *grave* mistake, damn right.

Nobody made a fool of Buford Muntz and lived to crow about it. Not if he was fool enough to leave Muntz breathing afterward.

The road felt like it stretched forever, nothing but the stagecoach tracks and hoof prints from their captured horses telling Muntz that they were even headed in the right direction. He lost track of how far they had walked since getting buffaloed, thirst eating at him from his parched throat to his burning eyes, the prairie sun relentless as it baked his brain with every step he took. Muntz started worrying, thinking that Drenen had been right for once, about the coach just rolling on toward the next town, dropping their horses there, maybe reporting to the local law where they'd come from.

In that case, without water, food, or firearms, Muntz reckoned they might be dead.

He wasn't giving up, though. Quitting ran against his nature, figuring he'd rather eat Drenen and Tutwiler than die out there from thirst and hunger. Something to consider, though it nearly turned his stomach at the moment.

Maybe later.

Luckily for his companions, only half an hour passed before Drenen cried out, "What's that I see?"

"Horses!" Tutwiler answered back.

"Figure they's ours?" Laze queried.

Buford Muntz could only roll his eyes at that, and mutter, "Goddamn idjit!"

Despite the interrupted highway holdup, Dempsey Poppert thought the coach was making fairly decent time. They'd got back up to speed once they had dropped the outlaws' horses and left their peculiar rescuer—Gideon Thorn by name—to make his own way at his own pace, with the pack mule trailing him. Poppert had put the bandits out of mind and concentrated on the road ahead of him, leading to Lazarus.

Barlow & Sanderson had no sales office there, as far as Poppert knew, and there was no point stopping. Their next station was another fifteen miles beyond the prairie town, a farm run by a character named Virgil Cribbs, where they would stop for water, feed the horses, and allow the passengers to use a privy if they felt the need. Nobody would be boarding, since the coach was full and no one had the Cribbs farm slated as their final destination.

That was funny when he thought about it, anyone on Earth wanting to spend their time with crusty Virgil and the small menagerie of animals he kept, including goats, chickens and ducks, a donkey, and a couple of alpacas he'd acquired somehow, from somewhere down in South America. The thought of stopping off to visit Cribbs and friends nearly made Poppert laugh.

Which might explain the pothole.

Poppert didn't see it up ahead and took no action to avoid it. When the coach's right-rear dropped down a good twelve inches, then rebounded, Poppert nearly lost his seat and Warren Mapes *did* fall, yelping in panic as he tumbled overboard and hit the dirt on his left side. The cry of fright became a squeal of pain then, Poppert hauling back his reins to stop the coach before they lurched and wobbled any farther down the road.

Poppert climbed down and ran back to his guard, ignoring questions shouted by the shaken passengers. He found Mapes sitting up, covered in dust, his right hand clutching his left elbow.

"You all right Warren?" he asked.

"Not hardly," Mapes replied. "My shoulder's dislocated, maybe busted."

Damn it!

"Lemme help you up, then," Poppert said. "We'll stop and see about a doc in Lazarus."

"Jesus, it hurts!" Mapes wheezed, but made it to his feet with Poppert's help.

"What did you say about another stop?" asked Eldridge Mottinger.

"Man needs a doctor," Poppert answered, brushing past him on his way back to the coach with Mapes.

The agent's wife called after them, "Haven't we wasted time enough already?"

"We'll be stoppin'," Poppert said over his shoulder. "That's an end to it."

"Well!" the woman huffed. "I never!"

I believe it, Poppert thought, but kept it to himself.

He helped Mapes climb onto the high seat, then ordered the passengers who'd left the stage to take their seats again. One of them, Delbert Akins, cautioned him, "You'd better check this wheel."

Shit fire!

Poppert climbed down again and walked back to the right-rear wheel, which he now saw was canted at an angle, flaring outward on its lower rim. He crouched beside it, peering underneath, and felt his stomach twist.

"Damned axle's bent, at least," he said. "It could be cracked."

"And what does *that* mean?" Mr. Mottinger demanded.

"Means you get back in the coach and we find out if it'll work. With luck, we'll make it into Lazarus and stop there for repairs."

"Stop there?"

"And if it don't work, we'll be sittin' here until someone comes along to help us out. Now get aboard, if you don't mind, or even if you do."

"My good sir..."

Before Mottinger could finish, Akins interrupted him. "Looks like we've got some company."

Poppert gazed back along the road and saw Gideon Thorn approaching, seated on his stallion with the pack mule following along and a bemused expression on his face.

The coach was able to proceed, which came as a relief, but only at a halting pace, groaning and rocking worse than ever with one of its four wheels out of line. Thorn rode off to the right and kept his distance, just in case the wheel came off and rolled away, turning the coach into a three-wheeled lump of wood and metal, going nowhere.

As the driver had predicted, they would have to stop in Lazarus, assuming they could make it that far, and find out if anyone in town could fix the axle. Thorn knew nothing of the stagecoach business except the obvious: tickets assured coach passengers of safe delivery within a given time, then listed various conditions that absolved the company of all responsibility for breakdowns, holdups, Indian attacks, and "acts of God."

In short, you paid your money and you took your chances.

He had listened to the passengers complaining—four of them, at least—but offered no suggestions beyond what the driver had in mind. The only other choice, as Dempsey Poppert had observed, was camping on the road and hoping someone happened by to help them out. As to what form that help might take, he couldn't guess.

So they were moving on and counting off the miles to Lazarus. Thorn had already planned to stop there overnight, if he could find accommodations and a decent place to eat. If not, he would have passed on through and camped beyond town, on the prairie, happy with a roof of stars over his head.

The town was larger than he had expected, when they reached it, but it couldn't hold a candle to the likes of Dodge or Lawrence, much less Wichita. When they pulled in, people appeared from shops and offices along the central street, closing around the damaged coach and calling questions to the driver. Thorn sat by on Shadow, watching Poppert brief the locals on their recent problems, asking for whatever help they could provide.

Within five minutes, maybe less, a lawman shouldered through the crowd, heard Poppert out, and started giving orders. "Somebody go fetch Doc Hornaby," he said. "And Cletus from the smithy, while you're at it."

Poppert bobbed his head. Said, "Much obliged, Marshal..."

"Farrell. Finch Farrell."

"If we're laid up overnight..."

"Don't fret about it. You're in luck," the marshal said.

"We've got a friendly town here. You can all fit in the Providence Hotel, our treat."

Thorn heard some of the passengers grumbling, but one of them—the fellow he'd pegged as a gambler—called out to the lawman, "Did you say no charge?"

The marshal smiled at him and said, "Seems like the only Christian thing to do."

LAZARUS, KANSAS

Thorn walked Shadow and Bell down to the livery while Poppert dealt with Dr. Hornaby, the marshal, and the mayor of Lazarus—a roly-poly man named Moody Grummond—while they got arrangements squared away. Poppert had said he'd bring the four-horse team along to join Thorn's animals when he was free, but Gideon decided not to wait for him.

The town had obviously been rebuilt since Rebel partisans ripped through the place eleven years ago, and had a certain air of newness that belied the passing time, with its exposure to the prairie elements. Most of the paint looked close to fresh, and Thorn surmised that people who have been burnt out before might take more pride in the appearance of their businesses and dwellings than would townsfolk who'd been left alone in peace during the war.

The livery was an example, clean and relatively fresh smelling despite the horses fertilizing half a dozen of its stalls. The smith who ran the place was busy with the stage downtown, but Thorn was greeted by a slender teenage hostler who'd been amply coached on what to charge and how to keep new patrons happy with his cheerful attitude.

In fact, the boy had offered Thorn free boarding for his mule and stallion overnight, but fair was fair, and since he hadn't suffered personally from the coach disaster, he paid up the standard rate of fifty cents per night for both. He helped unburden Bell, stacking her cargo in a corner of her stall, then took his saddlebags and two long guns, walking back toward the Providence Hotel.

Three stories high, the hostelry ranked as the second tallest building on Main Street, after the church, surmounted by its steeple with a six-foot cross on top. Thorn knew from reading history that it was not the first church built in Lazarus. Its predecessor had been torched by raiders with a fair number of worshipers inside, incinerating all of them in 1864. Gideon couldn't cite the final body count, but he knew it was crimes such as the sack of Lazarus that led Bill Anderson to ambush and a bloody death a short month after he had scourged the town.

Live by the sword...

The hotel's manager was somewhere in his early forties, with a tired and weathered face that aged him ten years at first glance. Only a second look revealed a sense of humor lurking in his eyes, but he restrained it as he welcomed Thorn and turned the heavy register around for Gideon to sign.

"You came in on the stage I take it, Mr. Thorn?" he asked.

"With it," said Gideon, "but not aboard it. It just happens we were traveling the same direction."

"Ah. Well, I suppose you're still entitled to the free room authorized by Marshal Farrell and the mayor."

"Word travels fast," Thorn noted.

"We're a small town, here."

"But since I'm not a stagecoach passenger..."

"I'm not about to buck the mayor and marshal, sir. They have the money in their city budget, I suppose."

"Well, if you're sure."

"No doubt whatever in my mind," the manager assured him. "Welcome to the Providence and Lazarus."

Thorn's room was on the top floor, overlooking Main Street. From its window he could look across at all the various attractions he'd expect a town the size of Lazarus to offer: a saloon they called the Glory Hole, a restaurant, a barbershop, a lawyer's office, and an undertaker's parlor. On his own side of the thoroughfare, as he had seen, there was the doctor's surgery, the marshal's jail, a hardware store, dry goods, and a museum dedicated to the massacre of 1864.

Must be for travelers, Gideon thought. Which local residents would want to be reminded of it on a daily basis, much less shelling out a dime each for the privilege?

Thorn, on the other hand, just might give it a look tomorrow, if the town offered enough to make him stick around another night. He had a passing interest in the stagecoach driver and his guard now, though he calculated one more day in Lazarus would be enough.

Boring or not, at least the hotel price was right.

FIVE

"It's gettin' dark," Laze Drenen grumbled.

"Funny how it does that every day about this time," said Buford Muntz.

"We gonna camp or what?" asked Elmer Tutwiler.

"Go on then, if you're weary," Muntz replied. "I'm ridin' on to Lazarus."

"What for?" Drenen inquired.

"Because that's where the stage went with our guns and them what owes us money."

Elmer asked him, "How you know they stopped in Lazarus?"

"Well, say they didn't," Muntz replied. "What else you look for in a town?"

"You're askin' me?"

Christ on a pony! "How about some booze?" he fairly snarled. "And maybe women? What about a gun shop? Could there be a nice fat little bank?"

"We ain't got that much money," said Tutwiler.

"Try to think once in a blue moon, will you?" Muntz

replied. "The last I checked, we was supposed to be outlaws."

"Oh, you mean—"

"Now you're gettin' it."

"That puts a diff'rent color on it," Drenen said.

"Glad you can see it, finally. And if the stage *did* stop for some reason," Muntz added, "call it Christmas in September."

It had taken them the best part of an hour to collect their horses, find their tack and saddles scattered in the grass, and get them fixed to ride again. Muntz truly didn't have the vaguest of ideas whether the stage would stop in Lazarus or not, but he supposed it might be possible, at least. And what about the solitary rider who'd disarmed him with his trick shot on the road? He was the one Muntz wanted worst of all.

That bastard owed him more than just a rifle. There was shame to be expunged, prestige to be recovered in the eyes of his companions, stupid as they were. Muntz had a reputation to preserve, although it hadn't traveled out in front of him the way he'd hoped when he first got into the bandit business. Far as he knew, he was only wanted in the eastern part of Kansas for some holdups and a shooting scrape where no one died. Enough to lock him up at Lansing's prison for a few years, but he wasn't in the same league with his heroes, Cole Younger and Jesse James.

Not yet, at least.

But if his luck held out in Lazarus...

Stagecoach or no stagecoach, he thought the prairie town still had potential for a good rip-roaring time that couldn't help but boost his name a few more notches up the wanted list. And maybe land him on the gallows too, one day, but wasn't that a risk that every bandit ran, the minute he picked up a gun?

Revenge and profit were the two best reasons Buford knew for doing anything. Put both of them together, and you had a pair of aces in your hand.

Too bad he had a pair of sloppy one-eyed jacks supporting him, but in the circumstances, they would have to do.

From the Providence, Thorn crossed Main Street to reach the only restaurant in Lazarus, a place called Adeline's. A waitress far too young to be the owner greeted him and led him to a corner table with two chairs. He scanned a menu printed on a chalkboard and decided on a twelve-ounce rib eye steak with fried potatoes, beans, and mushrooms on the side. It came with bread and started out with coffee strong enough to put hair on his chest, if he'd had any shortage there.

While waiting for his meal, he looked around the dining room and saw the stagecoach passengers dispersed at other tables, sitting two by two. One pairing looked to be a married couple, neither one excited by it or their impromptu adventures on the road. A second pair both looked like businessmen, one ten to fifteen years the other's senior, talking over plates of meat and greens in earnest tones. The last pair, male and female, didn't fit together well: Thorn had already pegged the male half of the couple as a likely gambler, while the woman had a certain style about her, shaded by a shopworn quality.

The driver straggled in just as Thorn's plate arrived. He spotted Gideon and raised a hand, then hesitantly made his way across the room. "Don't mean to interrupt your supper, Mr. Thorn," he said. "Just thought I'd tell you thanks again for helpin' us along."

"No thanks or 'Mister' called for," Gideon replied. "You want to sit?"

"Well... Hell, why not?" Poppert sat down, eyed Thorn's repast, and when the waitress came around told her, "I'll have the same."

Chewing a bite of steak, Thorn asked him, "Did the doctor patch your partner up all right?"

"His shoulder wasn't busted," Poppert said, "but he'll still have to wear a sling the next few days. He's restin' up at the doc's office now."

"And what about the coach?"

"The smith says he can fix the axle, but he can't start on it till tomorrow mornin'. It could take the best part of a day, meanin' we likely wouldn't leave till Sunday mornin'."

"And without a telegraph in town..."

"I can't report in to the company," said Poppert, finishing his thought. "Runnin' that late, I don't know if I'll have a job after we hit Topeka."

"They can hardly blame you for the holdup or a damaged axle."

"Wouldn't think so, eh? Thing is, Barlow & Sanderson, you never know. And if the payin' customers complain..."

"There's other stage lines," Thorn replied, knowing before he finished speaking that it sounded lame.

"Unless they blacklist me," Poppert replied. "I've seen it done before."

Arrival of his dinner seemed to put the driver in a slightly better mood. He dug in with a will, and none too quietly, eyes darting here and there around the dining room as if to see if any of his passengers were watching him, scheming to have him thrown out of his job.

"I can't believe we're stuck here in this godforsaken town," said Florence Mottinger, poking the food she'd barely sampled here and there around her plate.

"Tonight *at least,*" Eldridge replied, around a mouthful of what passed for meatloaf. "They'll be waiting at the reservation, wondering if something's happened to me. If I'm running out on them."

The very last thing that he needed was another dark blot on his reputation, even if it came by accident, through circumstances totally beyond his personal control. He cut a sidelong glance across the dining room, to where the stage-coach driver sat with their young savior, wolfing down his meal, and wondered how he could make life a little more unpleasant for the grizzled old-timer.

Servants were meant to *serve,* by God, not throw a wrench into the works and create problems for their betters.

"Eldridge, are you listening?" his wife demanded.

He hadn't been, and was in no mood to pretend. She'd gone along with his chicanery at Crow Creek, not apprised of any details, but insistent that he find ways to advance his lot in life. She'd never actually said *by hook or crook,* but must have had some inkling that the extra money they'd accumulated had been gained through underhanded means. No criticism from her at the time—that is, until the auditors came calling and revealed his perfidy. She didn't give a damn if Indians went hungry—if they died, for that matter—but when the shadow of his swindling fell on her, the carping criticism had begun.

How could he *be* so very stupid, after all? And underneath her sneering, his perception that she thought the *really* stupid thing was getting caught.

"Eldridge! I asked if you were—"

"Listening? Not really. No."

She blinked as if he'd slapped her, then pressed on. One thing about old Flo, shutting her up was damn nigh on impossible.

"I asked you if you thought this town seems odd."

"In what way, odd?"

"For one thing, I remember the itinerary at the depot."

"Station," he corrected her. "Railroads have depots. We've been riding on a stagecoach, if you hadn't noticed."

"Please don't be ridiculous! My point is that I read the schedule carefully and saw no mention of this Lazarus."

"Is that all?" Eldridge asked her, wearily. "Your great worry is having missed a town's name on the coach itinerary?"

"I did not *miss* it, Eldridge. I repeat to you: it was not mentioned."

"And the answer to your plight is obvious, my dear," he said, spearing another forkful of the meatloaf from his plate. "We weren't supposed to stop here, Florence. If we hadn't been attacked, and then the axle broken, we'd be miles beyond this dusty hole by now."

The waitress chose that moment to appear beside their table, asking, "Everything all right? With you, ma'am?"

"Perfectly delightful," Florence answered, showing her the stiff smile normally reserved for idiots and children, if there was a difference between the two.

"All right, then. Glad to hear it." The much younger woman bobbed her head and flounced away.

"And what was *that* about, Eldridge?"

"The waitress? Don't pretend you've never been inside a restaurant before. They *will* inquire if you don't eat your food."

"I'd hardly call this place a *restaurant*."

"They sell cooked food. It qualifies," he answered back. "Eat up. Your next chance will be breakfast, and who knows what that will be?"

"I'd hoped to have this meal in Wichita," said Julius Coffey, dabbing with a napkin at one corner of his mouth. "It's passable, of course, but—"

"How'd you get a leg up into politics, young as you are?" asked his companion, facing him across the table. Orin Pinkham came across as every inch a gentleman—or, at the very least, a gentleman who'd been required to ride a coach through dusty hinterlands, beset by troubles on the way.

And how should Coffey answer that?

Most people took for granted that a politician sold his soul to get elected. How could he explain, in diplomatic terms, that sponsors only *rented* it, and he was still his own man on the issues he regarded as important. Large donations purchased access, absolutely, but his mind was still his own.

Or so he told himself.

"We all start somewhere, sometime," he replied, smiling. "I've studied law but saw no prospects writing wills or helping neighbors sue each other down in Winfield. When I asked myself how I could make a difference for Kansas—"

"The state legislature came to mind," Pinkham chimed in, as if to answer his own question.

"I won't tell you it's the limit of my personal ambition," Coffey granted, hoping that he didn't sound too smug.

"It never is," Pinkham replied. "They're mostly farmers down your way?"

"Well, it *is* Kansas, after all."

"Oh, sure. But you'd need someone else behind you, right? A banker, I suspect, or maybe more than one?"

Coffey bought time by taking in a spoonful of his soup, some kind of bean concoction. What was Pinkham after, with this line of questioning?

"I'm not sure that I take your meaning, Mister—"

"Mister nothing. Call me Orin, will you?"

"Very well. But—"

"And I'm always looking for a good investment. Sometimes that means land, a piece of real estate. Sometimes it's a new business, getting off the ground. And sometimes it's a man."

"That's flattering, of course," said Coffey. "But I should remind you that I am a simple public servant."

"Aren't they all?" Had Pinkham *winked* at him, for just a second there? "Still," he went on, "it never hurts to make another friend."

Frowning a little, Coffey asked him cautiously, "What did you have in mind?"

"Thank you for sitting with me," Delbert Akins said. "I mostly eat alone, but never cared much for it."

"Living on the road's not easy," Laurel Dycus granted.

"Do you travel much, being a governess?"

She wondered whether he'd seen through her, wouldn't have been shocked to hear it, but she saw no signs that he was poking fun at her.

"It happens," she replied, working her cover story. Once you get out of Topeka, Wichita, and Salina, families that can afford someone to watch and teach their children are a rare commodity."

"You make a living, though," he said. "And my apologies, if that sounds like I'm prying into your affairs. I mean you no offense, in any way."

"None taken, I assure you." She was starting to enjoy his company but knew that there was nothing to it. She could spot a gambler coming from a mile away and knew she would gain nothing from attachment to him, even if it meant a pleasant night or two. Gamblers were married to their cards, their dice, whatever. As for Laurel, she had written off the dreams of marriage, picket fences and a family, so long ago that she'd nearly forgotten how it went.

Nearly.

"Where are you headed next, if I may ask?" Akins inquired.

"To Omaha," she said, "assuming that I ever get there."

"Ah. A thriving town, from what I hear."

"You've never passed through there?"

"Not yet. And someone's waiting for you?"

"Yes." He didn't need to know it was a madam named Maureen, who kept a stylish bawdy house downtown, a few blocks east of City Hall. They'd never met, but knew vaguely of one another, since word gets around.

"It must be nice," he said. "I mean, to be expected somewhere. Welcomed in."

"I won't be sure until I meet the family. They all sound good on paper, put their best foot forward."

"Well, I hope it works out for you."

"What about yourself?" she asked, surprised to find that she was interested. "Were are you off to?"

"Salina first, I guess. Then maybe up around Concordia."

"Well, if you're ever get to Omaha..."

Now why in hell had she said *that?* Laurel felt warmth rising into her cheeks and hoped the gambler couldn't see her blushing through the powder she'd applied in her hotel room, leaning close in to the antique mirror.

"I wouldn't rule it out," he said, and smiled at her again. "You never know."

When they finished with their meals, Thorn paid his tab and said good-night to Dempsey Poppert, then walked down alone to have a look around the Glory Hole saloon. It wasn't packed by any means, dusk come and gone on Friday night, but he supposed it was a decent gathering, considering the size of Lazarus. The place had a piano player, not the best he'd ever heard, and half a dozen sporting ladies that were standard for saloons throughout the West.

One of them saw Thorn enter, met him halfway to the bar, and looped her right arm through his left. A breast nuzzled his biceps as she asked him, "Are you new in town? I bet you came in on the stage."

"That obvious?"

"We don't get many strangers passing through."

"Not even going on to Hutchinson or Wichita?"

She shrugged. Another nuzzle. "Most of them take one look up and down the street, then keep on going," she replied. "You people breaking down's about the biggest thing that's happened to us in I don't know when."

"I wasn't on the stage," he told her. "It was just coincidental."

"But you're staying over, anyway?"

"It makes a change from camping on the prairie."

When they reached the bar, Thorn ordered two shots and a beer back for himself. The barkeep had a sallow, undernourished look, or maybe it was just the barroom's lanterns playing tricks. First glancing at him, Thorn had wondered when the man had his last meal.

The lady at his side—red hair, a corset cinched up tight to make the most of what Nature had given her—threw down her whiskey shot and asked him, with a crooked smile, "One more? Or we could just go on upstairs."

"I'll stand the drink," Thorn said, "but I regret to say this afternoon has sapped my energy for anything more strenuous."

"Hard to believe," she said, stroking his arm.

"You had to be there, Miss...?"

"Minerva. How's that for a corker? Most folks call me Minnie. What about this afternoon?"

"Just a long ride. It gets tiresome."

"Stopping holdups, too, I bet." She read Thorn's face and smiled. "Word gets around. You're like a hero. We don't get many of those in town."

"Nothing to get excited over," he assured her.

"But I *like* getting excited."

"Sorry I can't help you, there."

"You're sure? Not even for the anniversary?"

"Which anniversary is that?"

Before she had a chance to answer, the barkeep was

standing there and giving her the evil eye. "Minnie, ain't you got better things to do?" he asked.

"He bought a drink, Jed," she responded, peevishly.

"And sounds like that's the end of it. Go on and make your rounds."

Thorn wondered whether he should say something to that, but then decided not to rock the boat. He finished off his beer and tipped his hat to Minnie as she left his side. Settling his bill, he made a point of leaving off the tip.

Take that, he thought, and moved back toward the batwing doors as the piano player swung into "The Battle Hymn of the Republic," hitting maybe three notes out of five.

SIX

The three road agents straggled into Lazarus well after dark. There was no welcoming committee, hardly anyone abroad at all, though they could hear piano music and sporadic peals of laughter coming from a gin mill, somewhere down the street. They stopped dead at the town line, seated on their horses, sharp eyes roving up and down the street, probing at shadows.

"Don't' look like they're waitin' for us," said Laze Drenen.

"So? Why should they be?" asked Delmer Tutwiler.

"Just think about it," Laze advised him.

"What?"

"He means the stagecoach," Buford Muntz suggested. "If they come in talkin' about gettin' jumped, you might expect a lawman on the prod."

"Lawman!" Delmer leaned out and spat into the dirt. "I ain't afraid of one."

"You folded with that shooter, though," Laze said.

"Only because he caught me unawares. Bushwhackin' bastard."

"Wouldn't mind another shot at him, myself," said Muntz. No one was brave enough to mention that he hadn't got a single shot off in the first place, when the stranger had them covered.

"What? You reckon he's in down?" asked Laze.

"Don't matter. Goin' door to door around a strange place just means gettin' shot, sooner or later. And in case you didn't notice, we ain't fixed to do no shootin' back."

"I Thought you said we's gonna have some fun and make some money while we's here," said Elmer.

"And I meant it," Muntz assured him. "That don't mean we're gonna wander up and down the main street, callin' for whoever took our guns away this afternoon. First thing, we need to get ourselves some firearms."

"Marshal's office, if they got one," Laze suggested. Any law dog worth his salt should have a couple rifles and a scattergun, at least."

"And pack a pistol, too," Delmer reminded him.

"Lawmen ain't the only ones with guns out here," Muntz said. "I's thinkin' more about a hardware store or somethin' like it. New guns, all oiled up and pretty."

"Have to look around some," Laze stated the obvious.

"One pass should do it," Buford said.

"We walkin' in?" asked Delmer.

"Ridin'," Muntz said. "Case they spring a trap on us and we gotta skedaddle outa here."

Laze, sounding skittish, said, "Maybe we oughta just ride on and look for somethin' easier."

"Like what?" Muntz challenged him. "You wanna jump another stage with nothin in our hands but sticks and rocks? How'd that be?"

"Maybe find a farm," said Delmer.

"And when the old man comes out blastin' with a Henry or a Winchester, then what? You gonna tackle 'im?"

"Well..."

"Just forget it," Muntz commanded. "Guns first. Then we see what else they got to offer us in town."

"Guns first," Delmer agreed.

"Suits me," Drenen chimed in.

They started down the main street, didn't have a clue what it was called and didn't give a damn. Except for the saloon and the hotel, the other places lining either side were dark and shut down for the night. Even the marshal's office had no lamp burning inside, suggesting they had no one on watch or locked in jail.

Save that for backup, if they couldn't find a choice of weapons at the hardware store. Muntz saw it on his right, a fair-sized place, "Abrams" painted across the front, with mostly farm tools in the windows, targeting the local sodbusters. Guns would be farther back, maybe locked up the way some vendors did, with chain strung through the trigger guards.

"We need to go around in back," Muntz said, and pointed his overo stallion toward an alley on the near side of the hardware store. The others followed him as quietly as possible, alert for any signs of trouble, till they sat astride their animals outside the shop's backdoor.

"Be locked, I figure," Delmer said.

"Don't matter," Buford answered. "One way or another, we'll get in."

The clerk seemed glad to see Thorn when he got back to the Providence Hotel, almost as if he thought one of the place's new guests might have changed his mind about remaining overnight. He smiled and nodded, turned around to face the row of cubbyholes behind his counter, then told Thorn, "No messages."

"All right, then," Thorn replied, though he was not expecting any and had no idea how anyone on Earth, outside of Lazarus, would know that he was there.

"Good-night, sir!" Called out to him as he started up the stairs.

"Back at you."

"Sleep well!"

"That's the plan."

Thorn guessed it must get lonely, working night shift on the registration desk when no one came of went, but even so, the clerk was pushing it. Reaching his door, Thorn wondered if he should have stopped to ask about the anniversary Minnie had mentioned at the Glory Hole, and then decided that he didn't care. Some celebration of the town's foundation or whatever, and it meant nothing to Thorn.

Inside the room, door double-locked behind him, he took off his guns and thought about the disappearances in Colorado, and the long ride still ahead of him. The good news was, he didn't have to wait around until the stage-coach was repaired, but he was torn between immediate departure after breakfast in the morning, or another day of rest before he started on the westward trail to Breckenridge.

Another day or two should make no difference to his travels or the weather out in Colorado—snow wasn't expected for another month, at least, and then he knew the Rockies would collect it first. The gold miners who popu-lated Breckenridge would work on well into November, anyway, and if Thorn wasn't done with his research into the vanishings by then, he might as well give up.

The other question: what was there to hold him over for another night in Lazarus?

The town was nothing special, and while Minnie had a certain charm about her, it was nothing that he hadn't seen before in any number of saloons. What *did* intrigue Thorn was the barkeep stepping in and cutting off her talk about the local anniversary, as if it were some kind of secret only full-time residents were privileged to know about.

How odd was that?

Another explanation that occurred to him was simple jealousy. Maybe the bartender had eyes for sweet Minerva and he got a little antsy when she plied her nightly trade. If so, Thorn figured he should either find another job somewhere in town or make an honest woman of her, keep her close to home, where she could only use her practiced charms on him.

It hadn't felt that way, however, standing at the bar and watching them. The barkeep had seemed troubled, anxious at her blabbing, and when he had horned in on the conversation, Minnie had a look of fear about her.

Strange.

"And not my problem," Thorn said to his empty room.

No answer back to that.

Stripping for bed, Thorn finally decided he would make his mind up in the morning, whether to remain another night or pack up Bell and go. He would have breakfast first, maybe a haircut and a shave to hold him over on the road a while before he traveled any farther west.

And then, he'd see what he would see.

"How come I can't go sleep at the hotel with Dempsey?" Warren Mapes inquired.

The doctor—Perry Hornaby, his name was—had a long face that had mastered only two expressions Mapes could recognize: weary and sorrowful. He wasn't much on bedside manner, either, with his doleful looks and undertaker's voice, explaining things to Mapes as if he were a simpleminded child.

"I've tried to tell you," Dr. Hornaby replied, after a pause so long Mapes thought he might have missed the question. "While your shoulder is not broken, there is still a possibility of further injury if you exert yourself too much, these next few days."

"I asked you about sleepin', not exertin'," Mapes complained.

"If something happened to you at the Providence," Hornaby said, "I'd be remiss in not observing you or giving proper care. Their staff, such as it is, has no training for medical emergencies."

That frightened Mapes a little. "What kinda emergencies?" he asked.

"There is a possibility, though very slight, of some internal bleeding," Hornaby explained. "Swelling is the only warning sign, and if you are asleep, it might well go unnoticed."

"And what'd happen then?"

"If not immediately treated...well, it could be terminal."

"What's that mean?"

"You could die."

"Just from a shoulder jostled outa joint? You put it back already!"

"Yes. But if you had some knowledge of anatomy—"

"Gimme the basics, Doc. That's all I need."

"The human shoulder is a delicate and critical arrangement. There's the ball-and-socket joint, of course, also the clavicle—or what you'd call the collarbone. Injured muscles and tendons aside, you also have in there the brachiocephalic artery and vein, the subclavian artery and vein, all feeding into other veins and arteries along your arm."

Mapes felt his eyes glaze over as the sawbones rambled on with technicalities he didn't understand, but he was getting worried all the same. Who knew that falling on a shoulder and *not* breaking it could be so goddamned serious?

"Okay," he said at last, damming the flow of scientific terms. "I hear ya, Doc. Still seems like I could rest as well in a hotel room as I can with you, but if you're sure..."

"I'm absolutely positive," said Dr. Hornaby. "It would be totally remiss or me, perhaps even unethical, to turn you loose in your present condition."

Mapes half smiled at that. "Sounds like you got me caged, Doc."

"Not at all!" the medic hastened to correct himself. "If you desire to leave against my medical advice, and risk losing your arm or life, by all means go with my best wishes."

"Hey, now, not so hasty!" Mapes replied. "If it's that serious, I don't mind sleepin' here tonight, if you've got room. I oughta ask, though, what's it costin' me? Because Barlow & Sanderson likely won't pony up a dime."

"My dear sir, you're a visitor to Lazarus—and with our anniversary tomorrow, I might add. Consider application of my service as *pro bono*—that is, free of charge."

Mapes felt his smile expand at that. "Well, hell," he said. "The price is right. What kinda anniversary?"

"You likely wouldn't be familiar with it. Jus a milestone in our local history."

"Okay. And thanks, Doc. I could use some decent rest, at that."

In fact, Mapes wished he could have gone to the saloon, though he forgot its name. A drink or three would do more for his pain, he thought, than any of the doctor's bandages or fancy words.

"Sleep well, then," Dr. Hornaby said, as he left the little bedroom set aside for patients in his care. Before he doused the lamp he added, "Come tomorrow, maybe you'll feel fit enough to join us in our celebration."

It wasn't hard, cracking the backdoor of the hardware store. Kids could have done it, likely with their eyes closed, and the cheap lock posed no obstacle to Buford Muntz. Inside the place, pitch-dark, he fumbled toward the main room, Laze and Delmer almost treading on his heels until he stopped and hissed at them to keep their distance.

When they reached the sales floor, Muntz took out a match and struck it with his thumbnail, lighting up the place enough to see his way around. It only took a second for him to pick out a rack of long guns on the back wall, where the counter stood between them and potential customers. The glass-topped case in front of them held half a dozen pistols, mostly Colts, but with a Gasser Model 1870 from Europe tossed in for variety.

Before the march burned down to naked skin, Muntz was behind the counter with the long guns: Winchesters and Henrys, plus some shotguns, single-shot and double-barreled. They were chained together, as he'd seen in other stores, and Buford had to strike a second match to scrutinize the little padlock that secured the chain in place.

"Need somethin' that'll break this chain or tear it loose without a lotta noise," he whispered to his comrades. "Look around for tools and keep it quiet."

He had barely spoken up, as softly as he could in his excitement, when a voice he'd never heard before asked, "Can we help you out with that?"

Muntz spun around, dropping his match, but moonlight slanting through the store's display windows showed him the man who'd spoken. He was standing on the stairs that led up to his living quarters on the second floor, wearing a nightshirt and some kind of floppy hat that made him look ridiculous to Buford. Right behind him was a halfway pretty woman with long auburn hair, dressed in a nightgown made nearly transparent by the moon.

Well, now.

"You're likely wonderin' about us bein' here," Muntz said, trying to strike a reasonable tone.

"Oh, no," the woman said, not sounding worried in the least. "You're robbing us."

"I wouldn't put it that way," Buford answered, watching from the corner of his eye as Laze and Delmer started fanning out. Better to separate, in case the merchant had a gun he hadn't showed them yet.

"How else would you describe it?" asked the man, descending slowly with the woman close behind him. His attitude showed no more worry than the woman Muntz assumed to be his wife.

"We've fallen on hard times, is all," Muntz said, drifting a little closer to the staircase as his boys moved in. "The fact is, *we* was robbed. We need some of these guns to get our stake and horses back. When that's done, we can pay you for the use of 'em and somethin' extra for the trouble."

"It's no trouble, friend," the merchant said.

"No trouble. Not a bit of it," the woman echoed.

"So, you don't mind it we—"

Laze was close enough to make his move, leaping to close the space between him and the man they'd wakened. Buford didn't see the gleaming scythe until it struck, half-severing Laze Drenen's head, releasing gouts of blood that sprayed the nearest wall.

"No," said the smiling woman, holding up a twelve-inch carving knife, blade glistening by moonlight. "I can promise, we don't mind at all."

"You've made a hellish mess," said Reverend Hezekiah Gates. Light from the lamp he held reflected glints of crimson from the walls, floor, staircase—even from the ceiling overhead. It looked as if a madman armed with buckets of red paint had run amok inside the hardware store. The bloody fragments at his feet had once been three whole men.

"They tried to rob us in our sleep," said Martha Abrams, nightgown stained with blood from neck to hem. The worst part was the smear around her mouth.

"But you weren't sleeping, were you?" Gates inquired, rhetorically.

"The night before our anniversary?" John Abrams smiled, another bloody visage. Was there something caught between his teeth? "No, Parson."

"I don't have to say it, do I?" Gates inquired.

The couple hung their heads and answered him in something close to unison. "No, sir."

"I'll say it anyway: you've jumped the gun. I understand temptation. You may take my solemn word for that. But this is not how we do things in Lazarus."

Martha looked up at him and said, "They came upon us unaware."

"You *were* aware," Gates contradicted her.

"They meant to rob us, likely kill me, and do God knows what to Martha afterward," protested John.

"And you felt threatened...why?" asked Gates.

Their heads lowered again. Martha replied, nearly a whisper now, "The hunger suddenly came over us."

The minister released a pent-up sigh. "At last, the truth. How simple, and what great relief it is, to finally admit your sin."

"Are we forgiven, Pastor?" John asked, anxiously. "We didn't mean to jeopardize the anniversary."

"It's fortunate for you that these three did not come in on the stage," said Gates. "They won't be missed at breakfast in the morning."

John and Martha beamed their bloody smiles at him in obvious relief. "It's good to be forgiven," John allowed. "And come tomorrow—"

"Not so fast," Gates interrupted him. "Your penance shall be cleaning up the mess you've made—and I mean *thoroughly*. No trace of it must be discernible, come daylight. That includes the stains. If scrubbing or fresh painting is required...well, you *do* run a hardware store."

Their shoulders slumped now, but Gates noted looks of resignation mingled with the bloodstains on their faces. As he turned to leave, he asked them both together, "Were they tasty? Hot and juicy?"

"Oh, *yes,* Reverend!" said Martha.

"Absolutely, Pastor!" husband John chimed in. "I'd call them succulent, in fact."

"Not wasted, then," said Gates. "But you've been warned. No more indulgences before the celebration, or you'll pay the price for it."

SEVEN

LAZARUS: SEPTEMBER 25, 1875

Gideon Thorn rose early from a night of restless dreams that he couldn't recall upon waking. He thought there had been something about running, but with daylight breaking over Main Street, he could not have said whether his dreams were fearful or enticing.

When he'd groomed himself and dressed in black, from boots to high-crowned hat, Thorn listened to the call of hunger, exiting the Providence and striking off for Adeline's. Before he cleared the lobby, the same clerk from last night called out to him, "No messages!" Thorn wondered if he worked around the clock, then quickly put it out of mind.

He had his choice of seating at the restaurant, being an early bird, and chose a table at the window. From his seat, he saw assorted townsfolk circulating, some engaged in decorating shops with bunting, flowers, and the like, while four men worked at stringing up a banner across Main

Street. When they got it all stretched out, Thorn saw that it read "Happy Anniversary!"

A waitress came around with coffee, steaming, and Thorn didn't have to linger over choices from the chalkboard menu on the wall. He ordered fried eggs and potatoes, ham, and biscuits on the side with sausage gravy over them. Before she went back to the kitchen, Thorn inquired, "So, what's the anniversary?"

"Before my time," she said. "Something that happened in the war, I think it was."

If they were celebrating, Thorn decided, he might find out more about it, stick around for the festivities. The stagecoach passengers were stranded anyway, until their axle was repaired, and if the Providence decided Thorn should pay up for his second night, what of it? One thing his Aunt Drusilla had bequeathed him, in addition to her interest in all things spiritual, was more cash than Thorn calculated he could spend in two lifetimes. A night's rent wouldn't break him, and he might even enjoy himself.

His food arrived, and Gideon dug in just as the Mottingers began their walk from the hotel, across to Adeline's. First out among the travelers to meet a brand-new day, but neither of them looked excited by the prospect. She was talking to him, thin lips moving constantly, while he gave back terse monosyllables. They shut up altogether as they reached the restaurant and entered, eyes distracted as they skipped past Thorn and fond the menu on the wall.

"Sit anywhere you like," the waitress told them, coming back with Thorn's breakfast, and Mrs. Mottinger seemed to regard the greeting almost as an insult.

Used to being catered to, thought Gideon, and wished her husband well.

He dug into his breakfast, finding all of it delicious, with an unexpected spiciness about the sausage gravy. Thorn's ham, on the contrary, was almost honey-sweet. His egg yolks ran into the fried potatoes, and he didn't mind a bit.

Next stop, the barbershop. If Lazarus was celebrating, Gideon supposed he might as well spruce up a bit and get into the spirit of the day.

Marshal Finch Farrell made his morning rounds like any other day, but he could feel excitement thrumming in his veins. The anniversary was always special, and he played his part, such as it was, with pride.

The banner spanning Main Street was a new addition, whipped up overnight by energetic souls who'd used bedsheets for backing, three of them sewn end-to-end before the message had been painted on in gold, with silver outlining around the letters. Farrell spent a moment on the sidewalk, just admiring it, before he moved on, greeting shopkeepers at work on their own private decorations, offering congratulations to each one in turn on his or her specific handiwork.

Community was everything in Lazarus. It brought the town to life.

Farrell wore a tied-down gun but hadn't used it within living memory. The folks in Lazarus were law-abiding almost to a fault, which made his job, if not a pure delight, at least a restful sinecure. He made the rounds and showed his badge, but it was strictly ceremony, save when strangers came to town.

Like now.

There were nine new visitors, eight waiting in suspense

for Cletus Stokes to finish his repairs on their stagecoach, and one of them laid up with Doc Hornaby in his extra room. One of the nine was separate, although he'd come in with the others and the story was that he had rescued them from bandits on the road, just passing by coincidentally.

Good luck for them. Good luck for Lazarus.

The anniversary was meant for travelers, as much as for the town's abiding residents. It was an opportunity for citizens to share their story with newcomers, spread the word, and let the spirit of their settlement live on.

A legacy.

Finch Farrell reckoned he was fortunate to be a part of it, to lend a hand as needed, and to draw strength from the inspiration that accrued. How many frontier lawmen drew a blessing from the towns they had signed on to tame and keep secure?

Damned few.

As he moved along the sidewalk, smiling at his friends and shaking hands with those who were the most exuberant, the marshal knew he was a lucky man. Some other towns he'd worked in, prior to finding Lazarus twelve years ago, had been a trial and tribulation for a young official wet behind the ears. He'd learned his lesson in those other towns—and bore some of their scars, as well—before he found the place that suited him and settled down.

Crossing the street, he raised his face to feel the sun, smiling.

It was a damned sweet day to be alive.

The barber's name was Sweeney Flynn. He introduced himself, all smiles, when Thorn entered his shop and found no customers ahead of him. Flynn took his hat and black frock coat, hanging them on a rack beside the door, and eyed the white streak parting Thorn's hair from his forehead to the crown before he led his patron to the shop's one chair.

When Gideon was settled, with a drape over his front from chest to knees and tied behind his neck, Flynn said, "I'm not the nosy type, believe me, sir, but I'm obliged to ask—professionally speaking, as you'll no doubt understand—about that blaze across your scalp."

"A childhood injury," Thorn said. "It turned white overnight and stayed that way." He saw no need to mention being clawed by a demonic creature that had burst into his home by night and massacred the other members of his family. That part was private, but he recognized a barber's interest in quirky hair.

"Well, it's unique, sir. I can tell you that from thirty years experience."

"Some find it off-putting," Thorn said.

"People are strange about their grooming," Flynn replied. "Day after day, I see them sporting styles that make them look like circus clowns, and yet they'll talk to hell and gone behind somebody else's back about the other person's hair, whiskers, whatever it might be. It's part of human nature, I suppose, and not the best part. So, what can I do for you this morning?"

"Haircut and a shave," Thorn said.

"I'll get to trimming first and finish with the razor," Flynn explained.

"Sounds good. Can you give me the story on this anniversary you're celebrating?"

"It comes up once a year," Flynn said.

"Commemorating what?" Thorn asked.

"We had a tragedy during the war. Rebel guerrillas killed a bunch of folks and damn near burnt the town to ashes. Have you heard of Bloody Bill?"

"That's Anderson?"

"The very same. He was as bad as Quantrill, maybe worse. No pity in him, just an animal that lived to kill free-soilers. Met his end within a month of raiding Lazarus, I hear, and got what he had coming to him."

"So, you celebrate the massacre?" Thorn tried to keep his question neutral, not implying any criticism.

"No, sir! The town's rebirth from blood and ash is what we honor once a year. Bill Anderson and all his like can rot in Hell."

Thorn hoped he was imagining the barber's new indignant tone, accompanied by scissors snapping near his ears. Flynn finished up the trim in silence, then Thorn heard him sharpening his razor on a leather strop suspended from the backside of the barber's chair. Listening to the whisper of the blade on leather, he remarked, "It's good to celebrate survival anytime you can."

"You think so?" Now, instead of seeming angry, Flynn just sounded skeptical.

"I try to do it every day, in my own way," Thorn said.

The stropping ended, followed by a hiss of steam. Next thing Thorn knew, the barber had a hot towel wrapped around his lower face and neck. He left it there while mixing up the shaving lather in a mug, clink-clinking in the background, saying, "I suppose that's right."

At least he sounded calmer now. Thorn did his best to sit back and relax while Flynn applied the lather with a soft brush, covering the shadow of his two-day stubble. Seconds later, when the razor met his flesh, he tensed again, involuntarily, but was distracted from the moment by a shadow in the shop's doorway.

"You're keeping busy, Mr. Flynn," the new arrival said.

"As always, Reverend," Sweeney replied.

Thorn judged the new arrival to be six feet tall or thereabouts, clad in a gray suit with a black shirt underneath, its backwards collar designating him a member of the clergy. Set atop his head, a black felt pork pie hat made it appear as if his long face had been hammered flat above the lined forehead. Frown lines hemmed in his mouth like carved parentheses.

"You won't forget the celebration?" asked the minister.

"Not likely, Pastor," Flynn replied.

"Or start ahead of time, by accident?"

"No, sir." The razor's pressure on Thorn's neck eased up a trifle, then the blade began its first smooth journey to his jawline as the preacher turned and left the shop, proceeding on his way.

"I'll have you done here in a jiffy, Mister," Flynn announced, and started whistling as he worked.

Laurel Dycus breakfasted alone at Adeline's. She'd slept in later than she was accustomed to, and somehow missed the other stagecoach passengers, uncertain whether they had eaten earlier or would be dining later on this wasted travel day. Unhappy with the way she seemed to put on weight with her advancing age—though she was far from *old,* and damn whoever disagreed—she settled for a single egg, sunny side up, with toast and black coffee. If she felt peckish around noon, she could stop in for something else, or patronize one of the food stalls that were sprouting along Main Street for the celebration of their unnamed anniversary.

Her worries about age and weight came with the new job that she hoped was waiting for her somewhere down the road. Whether she found a whorehouse that required a sensible, mature professional to keep its girls in line, or if she started up a new one of her own, it always paid to look her best for patrons and the civic leaders whose approval she would need to stay in business.

And she wasn't getting any younger as the time slipped by.

Reverend Hezekiah Gates had spent most of the night in prayer, after he visited the hardware store to view the mess John Abrams and his wife had made. The fury sparked by their diversion from the plan had faded over time, was nearly dissipated as dawn broke upon their anniversary, but Gates meant what he'd said and would remind the other townsfolk as he made his morning rounds.

Whoever violated their tradition would be barred from joining in the ceremony. If he could, Gates would have banished them entirely from the town, leaving the dissidents to make their own way in the world alone.

Someday that power might be his, but at the moment his authority was limited.

Sunlight was warm upon his face and hands as Gates emerged from his white church and spent a moment on its steps, staring along the length of Main Street. Nearly all the decorations were complete now, every shop and office marked with some token that celebrated Lazarus, its history, and its endurance after passage through the flames.

Gates saw that some of his parishioners—and they were *all* his, on this day at least—had more imagination than their neighbors. But a celebration of this sort did not demand conformity, except in execution of the final ceremony at day's end.

For that, the town must come together, forged into a single unit with their one goal clear in mind.

Gates moved along the eastern sidewalk, pausing briefly at each door in turn, to offer blessings on the souls within and supplicating *Yeshua HaMashiach* to grant them strength. At some shops, the inhabitants came to him for a moment's heartfelt prayer. In others, where the occupants were briefly absent or engaged in some work out of sight, Gates simply left his blessing and moved on.

Not every town possessed the gift of Lazarus, to rise from smoking ashes and continue on. Most settlements of that size would have died out overnight, survivors scattered to the winds, their dreams forgotten, drowned in bitter memories.

Not Lazarus.

The bitterness remained, of course. It tortured Reverend Gates in solitary moments, wishing he'd been present when the wretched scum Bill Anderson was slain. He could have knelt beside the body, in the viper's blood, and prayed a rapid trip to Hell for Bloody Bill. Not that it would have mattered, since the Rebel trash was headed there regardless, but Gates thought it might have raised a crushing weight from off his shoulders.

Never mind.

They had the anniversary, and he would make the most of it.

His last stop on this side of Main Street was the Abrams hardware store. He had to see if John and Martha had obeyed his parting orders, purified their shop of any sign that they'd gone overboard and tried to start the celebration prematurely, on their own.

If they had not, he would be most displeased.

Dempsey Poppert turned up at the doctor's office unannounced. He bore a plate of breakfast he had bought for Warren Mapes at Adeline's, served in an old pie pan because they wouldn't let a dish go, covered with a napkin that had cost him extra: fried eggs, bacon, and potatoes with a biscuit, still half-warm after his walk down from the restaurant. He figured Warren must be hungry, didn't know what doctors fed their patients in a town like Lazarus, and thought he'd be the hero of the day.

First, though, he had to pull a little chain that rang a bell inside the doctor's residence, then wait for footsteps on the stairs inside, descending toward the ground floor level. Further waiting, till the door creaked open and the doctor stood before him in shirtsleeves, his vest unbuttoned.

"May I help you?"

"Come to see my pard and brung him breakfast," Poppert said.

"Ah, yes. You are the stagecoach driver?"

"Droppin' in to see my shotgun rider," he replied, thinking he shouldn't have to mention Warren's name. How many live-in patients could there be, a town this size?

"I have bad news," the doctor said, no change in his expression or demeanor as he spoke the dreaded words.

Poppert felt icy fingers clutch him by the nape. "He ain't...passed on?"

"No, no. But I admit to some concern over his lack of progress in the night."

"What's that mean, Doc?"

"You understand that any dislocated joint requires time to recuperate?"

"Yessir."

"But even so, having a good night's rest should bring the patient back to something like a normal attitude, except in the affected part."

"And Warren?"

"Virtually somnolent."

"Somno— Huh?"

"A heavy sleeper."

"Well, I brung 'im just the thing to wake him up, from down the restaurant." Poppert held up the pie tin, so the doc could catch a whiff of eggs and bacon. "Get this into 'im, he'll be as right as rain."

"I can't advise that at the moment," said the doctor, frowning as if he'd smelled something rank. "Frankly, in his present state, I'm not sure he could chew and swallow."

"Then I want to see him."

"Mister...?"

"Dempsey Poppert, speaking for Barlow & Sanderson's directors to call on their valued employee."

So he was stretching it beyond the breaking point. Too bad. It got him through the door, the medic's long face notwithstanding, trailing toward a kind of tiny bedroom where he spotted Warren stretched out on a cot, blanket pulled up around his grizzled chin, and looking pale.

"The hell happened?" he blurted out. "You give him something?"

"Nothing more than salicylic acid," said the doctor.

"What's that?"

"A mild palliative—that's a painkiller—for his shoulder, distilled from willow bark."

"It supposed to make him sleep like this?"

"No. That's unusual."

"What can you do for him?" Poppert demanded.

"At this point, we simply wait and see what happens next."

Cursing a blue streak underneath his breath, Poppert departed from the doctor's office, brain swirling and at a loss for something else to say. He took the cooling breakfast with him, thinking he could likely manage it himself.

EIGHT

After his trim and shave, Gideon Thorn dropped by the livery to check on Shadow and his pack mule, Bell. They both seemed fine and reasonably glad to see him, though the attitudes they both projected told him they would rather be abroad in Nature than cooped up inside their stalls.

One of the drawbacks to communicating with the so-called lesser species was that Thorn had to receive complaints and promise, when he could, to seek remediation. Satisfying both a stallion and a mule, he knew from past experience, could be a chore.

After the livery, Thorn set off to explore the rest of Lazarus. He wasn't shopping, needed nothing at the moment, but he browsed along the east side of Main Street, then started back along the west, reversing his direction. In the short time since he'd dined at Adeline's, he saw that nearly all the shops had sprouted decorations almost magically, not orchestrated or coordinated, but prepared by individuals with varied views about the anniversary of Bloody Bill's attack on their community.

Eleven years, and not a sign of it remained—which wasn't hard to figure, in the circumstances. Starting off from nothing, when a pack of rogues had burned it down, might be a painful task, but it also encouraged new ideas, new hopes and goals for the survivors of the raid.

After the other members of his family were killed, Thorn had been packed off to an orphanage in Lawrence, Kansas, where his Aunt Drusilla's manservant, Obi Magoro, had appeared to rescue him and carry Thorn away into another world he'd never dreamed of. Barely two years later, Lawrence had been sacked by killers who supported slavery. Seven more years had elapsed before another raid by Rebels—Bloody Bill that time, riding with William Quantrill—did even more damage to the city and its people, leaving well over one hundred dead.

Lawrence had managed to recover, but Thorn wondered whether, when their populations were compared, it might have suffered less than Lazarus. He didn't bother working out proportions in his head, but knew that for a smaller town to bounce back from nearly complete destruction was a feat rarely accomplished in the West.

"Oh, Mr. Thorn!"

The woman's voice calling his name made Gideon stop short and turn to see who'd summoned him. He picked out Laurel Dycus from the stagecoach, just emerging from a dry goods store whose doorway was festooned with wild-flowers he didn't recognize off hand.

"Miss Dycus, did you sleep well?"

"I was just about to ask you the same thing," she said, closing the gap between them, lowering her voice.

"Oh, yes?"

"Did you, by chance, hear anything *disturbing* in the night?" she asked.

"Disturbing? In what way?"

"Well...I admit that I was on the verge of sleep, sir, but I could have sworn I heard men *screaming* for a moment, not too far away from the hotel."

"Somebody coming out of the saloon with three sheets to the wind?" he offered, smiling.

Laurel shook her head. "No, I've heard that before. This sounded more like fear. And pain."

"Around what time was this?" he asked.

"Ten-thirty, going on eleven, I would guess. And not directly from the street outside the Providence. More like *inside* a shop nearby, and somewhat muffled."

"I confess to missing it," said Gideon.

"You're lucky, then."

"We could alert the marshal," he suggested.

"No. He'd only say I dreamed it and I'd feel a fool."

"In that case," Gideon advised her, "try to put it out of mind. He's coming toward us as we speak."

From the doctor's office, after gulping down his second breakfast of the day and wishing he had coffee with it, Dempsey Poppert tossed his pie tin in a trashcan standing up against the sidewalk's edge, next to a hitching post, and made his way down to the livery and blacksmith's shop. Across the street, he saw Gideon Thorn out for a stroll and nearly called to him, but then saw Laurel Dycus from the stage step from a shop and do the same. Rather than interrupt them with his news of Warren Mapes, he pressed on toward the forge alone.

He found the blacksmith, Cletus Stokes, just finishing his own breakfast. It seemed to be some kind of stew, served in a wooden bowl, and Poppert left him to it while Stokes got the last dregs scooped into his maw. When he had chewed and swallowed it at last, he turned and told the stagecoach driver, "I been workin' on your axle. May take longer than I thought to fix it."

"How much longer?" Poppert pressed him.

"If I worked all day and on into the night, it might be ready by tomorrow, sometime in the mornin'. Course, we got the anniversary today, and I can't pass on that."

"The ceremony," Poppert said. "I still ain't rightly sure what that's about."

"Survivin'," said the blacksmith. "Bouncin' back from when this old world knocks you down and tromps all over you, tryin' to snuff you out."

"I hear that," Poppert said, bobbing his head and swallowing a burp from breakfast number two. "But I was hopin' you fix the axle first and let us all get on our way, to keep my bosses off my back. You know Barlow & Sanderson, the company?"

Stokes shook his head. "Can't miss the celebration. Not for nothin'."

"How about for *somethin'*," Poppert asked him. "I could make it worth your while—or, anyway, my bosses could. They're always sayin' time is money."

"Works the same with me," Stokes said. "Except on certain special days."

"You're a religious man, I take it?"

"Passable, but nothin' to write home about. This ain't a churchy kinda thing."

"What is it, then?" Poppert inquired, suddenly curious,

since it appeared that he and all his passengers were going to be stuck in town for the fiesta.

Cletus Stokes smiled at him, but the blacksmith's eyes were far away. "It's more like gettin' back to Nature, and a *givin'* back, as well. Hard to explain for strangers. Anyway, you'll see it for yourself this evenin'."

"Yeah, I guess that's true," said Poppert, peeved to see his poor attempt at bribery rejected by the smithy.

"Don't you fret," Stokes told him. "Visitors durin' the anniversary are honored guests."

"Will there be drinks served?" Poppert asked. "I mean, you said it weren't religious."

"There'll be drinking, all right," said the smith. "Count on it. Everybody gets his fill."

"I guess that doesn't sound so bad."

Stokes grinned at that and said, "I wager that you'll be surprised. Now, I'll just get back on that axle while I have some time to spare."

Poppert turned from the forge and left him to it, thinking back to Warren at the doctor's office, damn near comatose. And from a dislocated shoulder? What in hell was that about?

He started back downtown, with no earthly idea of where he planned to go.

"Oh, hell," said Laurel Dycus, then she caught the look Thorn gave her, adding, "Please pardon my French."

"I've heard and said worse," he allowed.

She couldn't tell him that it had been bad news all her life, to see a lawman drawing near. In her experience, they either came to run her out of town, extort a bribe, or make demands for sneaky sex their wives wouldn't provide. In this case, all of those were out, since she was thought to be a governess and only passing through, but still she felt the same anxiety she'd learned to treat as a survival mechanism.

Now the lawman stood before them, tipped his hat to her, and introduced himself. "Finch Farrell, city marshal here in Lazarus."

She'd seen him yesterday and could have said the printing on his tin star told her all of that, except his name, but what she didn't need right now was any kind of argument or notice from the law. More reason not to mention what she'd heard—or *thought* she'd heard—from her hotel room's open window overnight.

Hell, if the citizens of little Lazarus were killing one another, it was none of her concern. She simply wanted out, on to the next city of any size, where she could look for work and get a fresh start under way.

"How are you folks enjoying our fair town?" the marshal asked.

"It's unexpected, Marshal," she replied.

He smiled at that. "Your stagecoach breaking down, of course. I understand. The good news is that you've arrived at an auspicious moment, with the anniversary today."

"We saw the banner," Thorn said, "and the other decorations. Talking to your barber, earlier, I understand it harks back to the war."

"Heard that from Sweeney Flynn, did you?" asked Farrell. "He sure loves to talk."

"I guess it comes with barbering," Thorn said.

"A woman's hairdresser is just as bad," said Laurel. "Gossip all the time, they do."

The marshal smiled and said, "Well, in this case,

Sweeney was speaking truth. That's not always his long suit, sad to say. I hope he didn't bend your ear too long."

"We got along all right," Thorn said, with what Laurel thought was just a heartbeat's hesitation.

"Good. That's good," the marshal said. "Because as visitors—by chance or otherwise—you're honored guests during our celebration of the past and future yet to come."

"No need to make a fuss about us," Laurel said, trying for bashful but afraid it might come off too stiff.

"And as for me," Thorn added, "I'm not with the stage at all, so—"

"But you were the hero of the hour," Farrell beamed, cutting him short. "That needs to be acknowledged, too. We're big on heroes here in Lazarus."

Thorn frowned and asked him, "What's involved in being 'honored,' now you mention it?"

"Don't worry," Farrell answered, seeming on the point of laughter. "You don't have to do a blessed thing but put in an appearance and enjoy the festival."

"Well, if that's all there is to it..."

"You have my solemn word," Ferrall replied. "The celebration starts at sundown. Until then, I hope you both enjoy our hospitality."

The marshal touched his hat brim as a parting gesture, stepped around them, and moved on. Thorn watched him go as Laurel said, "They take their celebrations seriously around here."

"I get that feeling, too," her young companion said, frowning.

Orin Pinkham woke with an uneasy feeling in his free hotel room, as if wriggling from the clutches of a nightmare he could not recall, bathed in a clammy sweat. He grudgingly released the satchel that he'd clutched throughout his sleep each night since fleeing from arrest—his only hope of building a new life, a new identity, wherever he wound up in his hurried, disorganized attempt to stay out of a prison cell—and sat up on his rumpled, sweaty bed.

The room was adequate, its price the best he could have hoped for, but it felt confining to him now, in morning's light. Not quite a cell, but close enough, the flowered wallpaper annoying him unreasonably in his sour waking mood.

Pinkham crossed to the vanity, poured water from its pitcher to a broad ceramic bowl—flowers on both, apparently a theme—and splashed his face repeatedly to drive the musty cobwebs of his bad dreams out of mind. He could remember times when all his dreams were hopeful, looking forward to the future. Now, they churned with dark foreboding and he spent his waking hours looking back, over his shoulder, for the law.

Surrender, then, a small voice in his head suggested. Just give up and make an end to it.

But that meant trial, conviction, prison, shame beyond endurance. Part of Pinkham knew his reputation was already ruined, shredded, trampled in the muck by newspaper reports, but he still clung to the belief that somewhere, somehow, hard cash money could secure him a fresh place in society. He could not change his face, unless he grew a beard, but names were easily replaced, biographies no more than spoken words requiring decent memory and certain bits of manufactured paperwork.

When he had managed to refresh himself somewhat,

Pinkham went back and sat down on the bed, reached for his bag—and nearly gasped aloud at how light, how *hollow* it felt. Sweating anew, he opened it with palsied fingers, gaped into its dark interior, and found nothing but shadows there.

His stolen cash was gone.

Impossible! He'd literally slept with the bag pressed against his chest since fleeing Kansas City, never took his hand off it or let it leave his sight while traveling. How could the money he'd accumulated from his depredation at the bank just disappear that way, without him noticing?

His first thought—wild, even deranged—was sleepwalking. Considering his recent spate of nightmares, might he not have risen from his bed of misery and placed the money somewhere else in an attempt to keep it safe?

A quick glance toward the door showed Pinkham it was double-locked. That strictly limited the scope of where his money might be hidden in the hotel room, and without hesitation he began to tear the place apart. He ripped the bedding free, first thing, then peered under the bed—nothing but dust mice there—before he moved on to the dresser drawers and then the closet, even turning out the pockets of his trail-worn suit and feeling down inside his shoes that needed polishing.

Nothing.

Panic set in, imagining what he would do—or, rather, what he *could not* do—without the money. First, he'd paid his stagecoach fare as far as Hays, Kansas, where he would need another ticket he could not afford and find himself trapped in a nowhere town, unable to acquire even the cheapest room or meal. Without the money he was destitute. Only a few coins in his trouser pocket rescued him from being literally penniless.

His mind raced feverishly, seeking explanations for the mystery. Who could have crept into his room, stolen the cash he clutched against his chest but left the satchel, then escaped while managing to double-lock his door from the inside? No one on Earth. His second-story window was not only locked in turn, but as he now saw, painted shut during some crude remodeling attempt. Forcing it open would be loud enough to wake the dead, much less a nervous felon on the run.

Tears struck him then, hysterical and furious. He curled up in the jumble of his sheets, knees drawn against his gut, and wept as if his life was over.

Which, as far as he could tell, it was.

Thorn parted company with Laurel Dycus soon after the marshal left them, wishing her a pleasant day and promising to see her at the sundown festival. He personally had no plans for the remainder of the late morning or afternoon, but sensed that she felt better on her own and had no wish to make his company an irritant.

Thorn had grown up without a governess, reserved back east primarily for female children or for families with more than one child to be tamed. His mentor and the best friend of his life, from his adoption to the present day, had been Obi Magoro, snatched from Africa by Aunt Drusilla's father sometime in Magoro's adolescence. Young he may have been, when taken captive, but he bore the tribal scars that marked him as a man full-grown and was adept at native martial arts including Dambe bare-knuckle boxing, Engolo ritual combat, and Nguni stick-fighting. He had imparted all of those to Thorn as need arose, in schools where Thorn stood out as "different" and thus subject to bullying. Today, though slowly aging, Obi still remained the bravest man whom Thorn had ever known.

And Gideon missed him each day, as he was traveling the West in search of mysteries to solve.

Now there was Laurel Dycus and the screams she thought she'd heard from her hotel room overnight. Thorn couldn't speak to the reality of that, but she had not appeared flighty, hysterical, unhinged, or any of the other frailties some men attributed in knee-jerk fashion to all manner of complaints from women. She was troubled by whatever she had heard, but that was all.

In fact, Thorn thought she'd held up very well for someone used to coping with the whims of wealthy parents and their spoiled brat offspring. He would have expected more emotion from the governesses he had met in passing, as a child and later on, rather than calm discussion of the strange nocturnal sounds.

Was it worth looking into? How would he even begin? The town's marshal seemed wrapped up in his preparations for its anniversary, and how would Thorn approach him without Laurel at his side to tell her story?

No. It was beyond him, a distraction that he didn't need or want to tackle now, when he was simply passing through. Tomorrow morning, early, he'd be gone from Lazarus for good, en route to Breckenridge, with Shadow under him and Bell trailing behind, long-suffering but prone to the occasional complaint.

And he would not be sad to put the town behind him. Quiet as it was, Thorn reckoned there was something *off* about the town, something that he could overlook for now, as he moved on in search of other riddles down the road.

NINE

Adeline's was crowded when Eldridge and Florence Mottinger sat down to breakfast, but the waitress served them promptly with their heaping plates of fresh, hot food. Regardless, Flo found ample grounds to criticize the meal, all of them boiling down to what her husband recognized from long experience: an inbred feeling that it wasn't grand enough for her, refined enough for her personal taste, and thus inferior at any price.

Which, in this case, was free of charge.

When he'd reminded Flo of that, she'd simply sniffed at him and snapped, "Which proves you get exactly what you pay for doesn't it?"

Despite the onset of another miserable married day, Eldridge had cleaned his plate and relished every bite of it, from fluffy scrambled eggs to ham wet cured in brine and sugar, buttermilk pancakes, and maple syrup that he could have sworn was freshly drawn. While Florence poked and muttered, he enjoyed. It was her choice if she went hungry, and he'd long since learned not to dispute her frequent sullen moods.

Leaving the restaurant, after she'd squabbled with him over tipping, they set out to see whatever Lazarus might hold for visitors. Her plan, of course, when Eldridge would have been much happier reclining in the hotel's lobby, reading a newspaper. Not that Flo was *interested* in the small town's offerings, by any means. She would be looking down on them throughout their walking tour, picking apart the shops, their merchandise, and any passersby in waspy language she reserved for her perceived inferiors.

Sometimes, Eldridge was troubled and embarrassed by the zeal with which he wished her dead and gone.

He missed the two young hooligans at first, when they stepped from the Glory Hole saloon into daylight, but they veered into his path, blocking the sidewalk and provoking Flo to make a clucking noise that sounded like a chicken in distress.

"Ex*cuse* us, if you please!" she said, before Eldridge could speak.

"And what if we *don't* please," the larger of the tipsy toughs replied. "What then?"

"I beg your pardon?" Flo replied, as she stepped back a pace from the onslaught of that one's alcoholic breath.

"I *said,* 'What if we *don't* please?' Whatcha gonna do about it, Missus?"

Eldridge knew that it was time to take a stand, even on shaky legs. "Now, listen here—"

"We's listenin'," the other morning drunkard said. "You got somethin' to say, Grandpa?"

Flo's eyes went wide at that. She made a little hissing sound, like steam escaping from a leaky radiator, then spat her favorite retort: "Well, I never!"

Giggling, the first thug answered back, "I ain't

surprised. Who'd wanna? Maybe you, Grandpa, if you was drunk enough to be half-blind?"

Eldridge's fear began a slow roll into rage. He'd never had a fistfight in his life, not even as a child—his father would have whipped him till he bled, whether he won or lost—but now he thought it might be unavoidable. He did his very best to sound manly as he replied, "Now, see here! You can't speak that way to—"

"Can't we?" said the second boozer, cutting off his stern retort. "Somebody told me this here is a free country, meanin' that I can say whatever goddamn thing comes to my mind."

The curse provoked another gasp from Florence, but she sensed the turn of things and held her tongue. Eldridge released her arm, which had been linked through his, and squared his shoulders, standing firm before their tormentors with fists clenched at his sides.

"Will you step back and let us pass?" he asked. "Or shall I—"

"What?" the taller of them challenged. "Whatcha gonna do, old man?"

Before Eldridge could answer, he looked past the pair and saw a third man stepping up behind them. Sunlight glinted brightly from the star pinned to his vest, as he inquired, "Is there some kind of problem here?"

Gideon Thorn watched from across the street as two young rips came reeling from the Glory Hole onto the sidewalk, intercepting the surprised and none too happy Mottingers. From where he stood, he couldn't overhear their conversation, but he got the gist of it all right: the rowdies meant to have some drunken fun with strangers, and the Mottingers were in high dudgeon, wanting none of it. The drunks, as he had learned from past experience, were quick to take offense, even when they had caused the problem to begin with.

That spelled trouble, and he was about to cross the street when he saw Marshal Farrell coming up behind the drunks. Before they'd noticed him, he said something that seemed to halfway sober up the miscreants. Thorn watched their heads bob, both delinquents taking off their hats in what he took to be a gesture of respect, however feigned, for Florence Mottinger. Another moment, and the married couple moved along, Farrell remaining with the drunks after they'd gone.

Thorn wished he could have listened in to Farrell's words, as he stood watching their result. The trouble-makers—maybe brothers, from the look of them—stood now with shoulders slumped and eyes downcast, taking the lecture he delivered without talking back. Long moments passed, before Thorn saw the minister he'd glimpsed that morning from the barber's chair, straight razor pressed against his throat, approaching from behind the marshal. They had words, and then the preacher lit into the drunkards on his own account, both of them shriveling before his discontent.

Thorn thought back to the barbershop and how the razor felt against his skin, as if about to disobey the barber's hand and bite into his throat, seeking the jugular, before the minister appeared in the doorway and spoke the simple words, "You're keeping busy, Mr. Flynn." There'd been some kind of undertone to that, which Thorn couldn't identify, but it had changed the barber's mood in nothing flat, as if he'd been caught doing something wrong.

He watched the preacher now, chastising two young men without the need to mince his words, and glimpsed a measure of the power he exerted over his parishioners. Not that Thorn would have pegged the drunks as church-goers, by any means, but they seemed more impressed by harsh words from the minister than from the marshal, who could simply have arrested them and locked them up.

Peculiar, certainly, but Thorn couldn't explain exactly *why*.

Another riddle, but it didn't fall within the range of what he normally investigated as he roamed across the West. Screams in the night that might have been a dream or drunken revel at the Glory Hole, and now a preacher lambasting two boozers. There was nothing for him here, as far as he could see.

In fact, Thorn wondered whether he should go back to the livery, retrieve his animals, and leave right now, but he was getting hungry and it put him off the road.

"I might have known," Finch Farrell said. "The Mowbray brothers, drunk again."

"We didn't do no harm, Marshal," Mike Mowbray said, the older of the pair. "Just havin' fun."

"Just havin' fun," his brother Merton echoed, which was common for the simple-minded sibling.

"Fun? Harassing special guests this soon before the celebration? You let red-eye do your thinking for you."

"Marshal, that ain't fair!" said Mike. "We're just gettin' a little jump on it, that's all."

"That's all," Merton agreed, nodding.

"And if they didn't like your little prank, what then? You plan to beat them up, or worse?"

"They started gettin' lippy with us," Mike protested. "We don't have to take that from some puffed-up city folk!"

"I'm lipping off to you right now," Farrell replied, cold-eyed, his right hand resting on his holstered Peacemaker. "You want to do something about it?"

"Marshal, come on, now."

"Come on," Merton mouthed, seeming near tears.

Farrell knew he was getting riled beyond the situation's need, but it felt right, felt *good*. He craved the anniversary's release as much as anybody else in town, wishing that he could set the clock forward and move the sun across its sky toward dusk. "The last thing that we need," he fairly hissed, "is trash like you two spoiling things for everyone. I ought to—"

"Do we have a problem here?" a deep voice from behind him asked.

The lawman turned and blinked at Reverend Gates, eyeing the three of them. He seemed to recognize the situation without being told, but Farrell summarized it for him anyway, laying the blame squarely on Mike and Merton Mowbray, and their love of booze.

Gates listened, scowling as he often did, and said, "You two have risked the celebration's sanctity. You understand the consequences of your actions if you'd followed through?"

Heads bobbed again. "We do, Pastor," both brothers said, as one.

Gates couldn't let it go at that, of course. He pressed on. Said, "Because you would be cast into the outer darkness, never to return. Your fellowship with Lazarus and with each other would be lost forever. Is that clear?"

"Yes, sir!" they volleyed back, no telling who had echoed whom.

"Now go about your business, mind your manners till this evening, and for God's sake, sober up!"

The Mowbrays scuttled off, chastened, as Farrell felt eyes boring into him. He turned and glanced across the street, to find the so-called hero from the stage holdup regarding him and Pastor Gates with pointed curiosity.

"We have an audience," he told the minister.

Gates pivoted his head alone, boots planted firmly on the sidewalk, nodding almost affably to Thorn. "That one could be a difficulty," he told Farrell, thin lips barely moving as he spoke. "There's something about him. I don't know what it is, but I smell trouble."

"He could have an accident ahead of the festivities," Farrell suggested.

"Don't be hasty," Gates replied. "I want to see what happens next, and nothing should upset our other guests before they play their roles."

"Just as you say, Pastor."

Gates left him then, without another word. An order had been passed, and Farrell would obey it. If the ceremony was disrupted, it would not be his doing, and no one in the town could say he had not offered a solution to the minister, only to see his plan turned down.

When he calmed down enough to dress himself, Orin Pinkham thought maybe he should tell the law in Lazarus about his missing cash. And having thought that, he immediately canceled out the notion, realizing he could not explain where so much money came from in the first place, any more than he could tell the marshal where it went.

Involving the authorities would raise an instant question about provenance, and then possession, of the funds he had embezzled from his bank. It wouldn't take much research for the marshal to uncover wanted posters naming Pinkham as a thief with warrants out against him in Missouri. He could not explain that, even if he tried, and he would land in jail before he had a chance to spin whatever tale his mind might manufacture. Next came extradition, which he would resist if he could find a lawyer prone to work for free, but it would be approved within a week or two. Then back to Kansas City for his trial and all that followed afterward, unless he somehow found the nerve to kill himself.

Pinkham considered that right now, a grim alternative, but maybe better than the shame that followed hard behind exposure, criminal conviction, and imprisonment. It seemed a certainty that he would die in jail, regardless of the sentence handed down. Cast in among the savages, how could he last a month, much less for years on end?

And if he *did* survive to make parole, what then? He would be flat broke, unemployable as an ex-convict found guilty of theft. No one would trust him with the lowest job at any business, much less a post on par with the position he'd defiled.

"As good as dead," Pinkham muttered, and thought about the razor in his shaving kit, which had not been disturbed by last night's thief.

What did it matter if a hotel maid walked in and found him dead by his own hand, blood soaking through the sweaty sheets and mattress on his bed? No one would miss him but Missouri manhunters, and they would only spend the time required to call in posters on him, wrapping up the hunt. He'd be forgotten in a week or two, except by the depositors he'd robbed in Kansas City. They could come to Lazarus and piss on Pinkham's grave for all he cared.

But then the problem reared its ugly head again. He didn't have the nerve to use the razor on himself and didn't have a pistol in his suitcase. He was terrified of heights, and leaping from his second-story hotel window likely wouldn't kill him anyway. He'd go to trial and into prison as a cripple, easy prey for any convict on the prowl.

His stomach growled, and Pinkham suddenly remembered that the meals were free for stranded stagecoach passengers in Lazarus that day. Come sundown, he could eat more at the anniversary party, and maybe even drink his fill. Would alcohol provide the guts he lacked when sober, all that was required to end his worthless life?

He could but hope.

Donning the jacket to his wrinkled suit, Pinkham went out—leaving his satchel for the first time since he'd stuffed it to the seams with cash, back in K.C.—and started his descent to Main Street, hoping Adeline's would still be serving when he got there.

The breakfast menu had been scrubbed and written over with a list of offerings for lunch when Thorn walked into Adeline's. He took a seat facing the street, back to a wall, and ordered chili with a slab of fresh-made cornbread on the side. It reached his table within minutes, piping hot, the chili a surprising mix of beef, pork sausage, beans, tomatoes, onions, peppers red and green, all thick enough to let his spoon stand upright in the middle of it, on its own. The cornbread steamed and butter melted almost instantly on contact with it, soaking through the small loaf that included jalapeño peppers mixed with corn. The combination set his mouth on fire, but Thorn quenched it with ice-cold beer.

While he ate, Thorn watched the flurry of activity continuing on Main Street. There was no doubt that the residents of Lazarus—should he call them Lazurians?—were totally committed to the celebration of their quasi-tragic anniversary, complete with bunting and window displays of merchandise discounted for the special day. He'd never seen a frontier town approach a civic celebration with such zeal before. In fact, it brought to mind some of the holidays he'd witnessed growing up in Boston: Saint Patrick's Day for Irishmen, especially, and Saint Stephen's Day among Italians, falling one day after Christmas.

Everyone he saw outside appeared to have the spirit stirring in them, making preparations, looking forward to the party scheduled to begin at sundown. Thorn still had no clue what that entailed, but he was curious.

Another point of curiosity, less casual, involved the seeming change in attitude among some townspeople as time progressed on Saturday, with morning slipping into afternoon. Some of them were starting to seem over-wrought—was *angry* too strong a description of them?—as the celebration of their special day drew nearer. He had discounted the peculiar incident outside the Glory Hole saloon, between two drunken locals and the Mottingers, but now Thorn wondered if he ought to reconsider that. Across the street, he saw the politician from the stagecoach, Julius Coffey, walking down the sidewalk, window shopping, and it seemed to Thorn that several of the Main Street merchants dropped their cheery smiles as he passed by, their faces shifting into bitter scowls.

More morning drunks? Thorn doubted it, but neither could he figure out why anyone in town would glare at Coffey nor at any of the other stagecoach passengers selected, quite against their conscious will, as honored guests for that night's festival. It seemed incongruous and inexplicable.

That brought him back to Laurel Dycus and the screams she's heard or dreamt on Friday night. If she was right about the sounds, what did they mean—and what did they portend for Saturday, after the sun went down?

It was too much for him to contemplate right now, stray pieces of a puzzle where the vast majority of bits were missing and he had no earthly clue as to the final scene depicted by the finished work. It seemed, in fact, to be a futile waste of time, buy it still nagged at Thorn as he finished the remnants of his meal, paid up, and went back to the sunny, decorated thoroughfare.

TEN

The town leaders of Lazarus convened in special session at the Holy Resurrection Chapel on Main Street. Reverend Gates presided from his simple pulpit, decorated only with a hand-carved crucifix some three feet tall. Facing him from the first pew sat Mayor Moody Grummond, Marshal Finch Farrell, and Dr. Perry Hornaby. Their mood was solemn, but a close observer might have noticed that the trio in the pew all seemed to quiver with anticipation where they sat.

"This is our final gathering before the ceremony," Gates intoned, stating a fact well known to all of them. "When next we meet as one, the celebration shall be under way."

"If some in town can wait that long," said Marshal Farrell.

"Has there been an incident?" Gates asked.

"You saw the Mowbray brothers," Farrell answered him. "It was a good thing for that couple from the stage that I showed up in time, and you behind me."

"I expect no better from the Mowbrays," Gates replied, to knowing looks and nods from Mayor Grummond and Dr. Hornaby. "They'd stay drunk all the time if that were possible, and rarely give a thought to anything they do. I've cautioned them, explained the consequences if they misbehave again. My hope is that they'll take my words to heart."

"It's not just them," said Farrell. "I've been out there on the street, and you can feel the spirits turning if you pay attention. Folks are working up a bigger head of steam this year, some of them getting mad where you can see it leaking out. I don't know whether it's the wait till sundown—"

"Absolutely critical," the minister reminded him.

"Or if there's just too many strangers roaming around town this time, stirring things up. Whatever, I can try to keep a lid on it, but without deputies, I can't be everywhere at once."

"We share responsibility," said Gates. "Mayor Grummond can assist you on patrol, yes?"

Grummond looked surprised at that but made no protest, simply nodding in a way that made his double chins wobble.

"And Dr. Hornaby—"

"I have a patient at my office, Pastor," Hornaby cut in. "I have him partially sedated, though his injuries do not require it. Leave aside his injured shoulder, and he should be fit as any of the others."

"But...?" Gates prodded him.

"His friend, the driver, obviously wants his partner with him when they leave tomorrow. He's already stopped in once to check on him."

"Tomorrow?" Pastor Gates actually smiled at that. Grummond and Farrell picked up on his mood, the joke behind it, chuckling to themselves. "What difference does that make, Doctor?"

Hornaby came close to blushing, dipped his head, and

said, "Of course. But in the meantime, there could still be trouble from them."

"And we're trusting you to deal with it appropriately," Gates replied.

"Yes, sir."

Gates could have told his three associates about the Abrams Hardware incident last night, but what would be the point? They suffered from a measure of uneasiness already, fear that something would disrupt the festival. Why should he worsen that condition with his news about three strangers—common criminals, at that—who'd set off something in John Abrams and wife Martha, suffering the very fate that they deserved. The three strangers had not been honored guests, so nothing was detracted from the anniversary's climax. Best not to mention them at all and rock the boat unnecessarily.

If there were any further incidents, he would deal swiftly and decisively with those involved. Until then, Gates had no reason to borrow trouble on this Day of Days.

Gideon Thorn decided that the best place for a test of moods in Lazarus would be the Glory Hole saloon. He entered through the batwing doors, piano music jangling at him, and surveyed the room before proceeding to the bar. Off to his left, he picked out Delbert Akins from the stage, playing a game of five-card draw with four men Thorn assumed were local residents. None of the players wore a jovial expression, and the pile of chips in front of Akins was the smallest on the round table.

Losing, which would explain the gambler's frown, but Thorn could not account for matching grim expressions on the faces of the winners. Maybe, he decided, men in Lazarus were prone to take their poker seriously.

A tall and long-faced barkeep took Thorn's order for a beer and left him sipping it to deal with other customers. For one o'clock, albeit on a Saturday, Thorn was surprised by all the customers drinking and gambling in the Glory Hole. He counted close to forty of them, several clearly drinking to excess, but none competed with the out-of-tune piano with their conversations. There was none of the well-oiled hilarity he'd come to know from other bars across the West.

In fact, it almost seemed as if the Glory Hole's patrons were in a state of mourning, trying to decide if grief or anger was the proper mood. All Thorn could think was that it had to be the anniversary of Bloody Bill's attack on Lazarus, reminding all its present citizens of what had happened just eleven years ago—and could, at least in theory, repeat itself if they were targeted by Indians or prairie outlaws sometime in the future.

But in that case, why a celebration? Why not let the date pass by, no special notice taken of it till the anniversary had passed once more and yet another year replaced its memories of slaughter?

Thorn could not account for local feelings, much less for the qualities of memory the small town chose to cultivate. More to the point, it was none of his business. He would watch the sundown ceremony for a while, and if it seemed to take an ugly, drunken turn, he would retire to his room at the Providence Hotel. Leave in the morning, early—or before then, if it came to that, retrieving Bell and Shadow from the livery.

As Thorn worked on his beer, he noted several other patrons casting sidelong glances at him, trying not to be conspicuous. Among their number, he included two men standing at the bar, both total strangers to him, and some others seated round the tables at his back, faces reflected in the backbar mirror while Thorn kept his eyes forward and seemed to concentrate on drinking.

And so what?

He was as strange to the Lazurians—the term he now had stuck in mind—as they and their town were to him. His garb, all black from head to toe except his shirt, with guns on either hip, besides his Bowie knife and dagger in his boot, would have drawn notice from the crowd in any bar, no matter where he went. If Thorn acknowledged it, he had a lethal look about him, earned in equal parts from things that he had suffered as a child, things he had seen as an adult, and things that he had done to keep himself alive during his travels up and down America's frontier.

He was an unknown quantity, and one that radiated danger warnings to suspicious strangers on the road. Toss in an anniversary that seemed to carry sour memories for many townsfolk, and he couldn't let his mind fasten on wild imaginings about the mood in Lazarus.

But it was getting underneath his skin, and there was no denying it.

Del Akins barely noticed Thorn when his rescuer from the day before entered the Glory Hole. His eyes and mind were focused, rather, on the sixth straight rotten hand he had been dealt since sitting down to play a friendly, hopeful game of five-card stud with total strangers in the bar.

The deal had passed around while they were playing, landing once on him, and even then he couldn't seem to stir up any luck. The other players, names forgotten within seconds of their introductions, dealt methodically, almost mechanically, and if they had a scheme to cheat the only stranger at their table, Akins couldn't catch them at it—a surprise, since that was more or less his specialty.

This time around, he held an ace of spades, not bad, but all the rest of it was shit: a deuce and six of hearts, a queen of diamonds, and a ten of clubs. He couldn't build a straight from that, much less a flush, and at the moment didn't even have a lousy pair.

The ante was a dollar, but he felt a little better as the other players went around the table from his left, checking instead of placing any bets. Time came for them to discard their unwanted cards and draw replacements, making Akins wonder what they'd think of him if he ditched four and only kept the ace? Would they know he was ripe for picking? Would his tardy luck step in, reward him with a hand he could be proud of after losing twenty dollars as it was?

He waited for his turn, discarded four, and watched the dealer hand him four new cards. None slipping from the bottom of the deck, no dealing seconds, nothing he could spot from staring at the dealer's blunt, rough hands. When he had all four cards, Del scooped them up, fanned them— and had to work at keeping up his deadpan poker face.

Against all odds, he'd drawn the ace of clubs and three eights: hearts, diamonds, and spades. He held a full house now, third highest winning hand at poker, and the sight of it elated him, the way farmers must feel when rain begins to pour during a savage drought.

Now, all he had to do was wait for betting to begin, circling the table from the dealer's left. This time, each of the other players laid down wagers, growing as they went around the circle, raising bets that came before. Del waited for his turn, and when it came, frowned at his cards as if he wasn't sure exactly how to read them.

When he felt the others getting restless, he relieved them with a little shrug, then pushed the remnant of his chips into the pot, saying, "All in."

Mildly astonished faces studied his, then from the dealer onward, one man at a time, the others matched his bet. Akins counted two hundred fifty dollars in the pot, enough to walk away with if he didn't feel the need to stay and try for more.

"Let's see 'em," said the dealer.

Akins laid his cards out on the table, didn't bother to explain them, since their faces told the tale. Three of the others slumped, tossed in their beaten hands without revealing them, but then the player facing him directly started dropping cards one at a time. Del watched him, picking out the six of clubs, the six of hearts, the six of spades, the six of diamonds, and a useless jack of spades. He didn't need to hear the victor's voice pronounce his doom: "Four of a kind."

It was the *second* highest poker hand, defeated only by a rare straight flush. Akins was busted, broke, except for small change shifting in his trouser pocket, all the money he still had left to his name.

He tried to put a brave face on it—never let them see you run off, blubbering—nodding congratulations to the man who'd gutted him and rising from the pasteboard battlefield, telling them all, "That's it for me. Thanks for the game."

His churning mind spat *Thanks for goddamn nothing,* silently, as he retreated from the Glory Hole and out into the blinding sunlight of a day gone hopelessly and hideously wrong.

Julius Coffey, tired of Main Street and its decorations, broiling underneath a prairie sun, retrieved his room key from a pocket of his vest and let himself into his room. Someone had tidied up while he was out, but it was still as plain and drab as he remembered upon checking in. How could a legislator for the State of Kansas be reduced to this by what some might have called an act of God?

He latched the door behind him, force of habit when he traveled, no real worry of intruders bursting in on him, and loosened his necktie. He wished the Providence Hotel had baths available for guests, but then, on second thought, grimaced while wondering how often public baths were cleaned, how thoroughly their porcelain was scrubbed.

Better to sweat a while, and face offending his collected stagecoach partners in the morning, than to brave the risk of an infection from facilities improperly maintained, with no attention to hygiene.

He was unbuttoning his coat when something *shifted* on his made-up bed, beneath the comforter. Frowning, Coffey approached, picked up a corner of the spread, and tossed it toward the footboard—leaping backward as a fat diamond-back rattler was revealed, coiled for a strike, hissing with the sibilance of sudden death.

He was unarmed, had no idea how to respond, but was retreating toward the latched door when he heard more rattling from the dresser to his left. A glance showed him another serpent coiled there, in the empty water basin, and he saw the dresser's top drawer *moving* now, as something trapped inside it struggled to escape. Before his very eyes, a third rattler appeared, head rising from the aperture its writhing coils had opened.

On the floor, barely six feet away from him, a fourth and firth snake spilled from underneath the bed, tongues darting in and out, their rattles joining in an arid symphony of stark mad raving fear. Five pairs of eyes were focused on him, their elliptical pupils narrowed to slits like gunsights aimed at Coffey from around the room.

He fumbled backwards for the doorknob, found he could not turn it, and forgot the simple locking mechanism in his abject terror. Loudly, hopelessly, the newest Kansas lawmaker began to scream.

Gideon Thorn, well fed and sun-baked from the street, had almost reached the door of his hotel room when a scream shattered the hallway's stillness, echoing with banshee strength inside the corridor. It took another moment for him to decide which numbered door concealed the screamer—obviously male—then he rushed toward it, knocking loudly as he called out, "Who's in there? What's wrong?"

He heard a frantic scrabbling on the far side of the door, like fingernails, and saw the doorknob shake, as if someone were twisting it in vain. "If you can't open it," he shouted, "step back from the door. I'll kick it in."

"Can't move!" a voice he vaguely recognized cried out. "They're everywhere!"

They? What in hell was happening?

"All right," he told the hidden man. "I'm kicking it."

Thorn raised his right leg for a strike beside the knob,

the best place for a hit to snap cheap locks, and was about to let it fly when, suddenly, the door flew open as if on its own. One of the stagecoach passengers—the politician, Coffey—spilled out of the room and clutched Thorn's shoulders, ashen-faced, eyes wild.

"Don't go in there!" he warned. "The snakes...my God...where did they come from?"

Thorn sidestepped the trembling man and drew his right-hand pistol as he eased his way into the hotel room. It had a musty, ancient leather smell about it that he barely recognized, but nothing else seemed out of place except a comforter, thrown back and draped across the bed's footboard.

He scanned the room for any sign of shifting move-ment, stooped to peer beneath the bed, then turned to Coffey standing in the doorway and inquired, "What snakes?"

"Jesus, just look at them!"

Coffey followed his own advice and leaned into the room, head swiveling, at once discovering what Thorn had seen.

Nothing.

"But they...I swear I saw them! There were five, at least, huge diamondbacks." He turned to Thorn, face stricken, eyes brimming. "Jesus! Where did they go?"

Thorn poked around a little more: nothing below the dresser or in any of its drawers, nothing but hanging clothes inside the chifforobe. "I don't see anywhere at all for them to go," he said.

"But...how?" Scanning the empty room, Coffey stepped back across the threshold, peering high and low, his face passing from terror to abject mortification. "I don't under-stand. I'm sure I saw... Oh, God! You must think I'm insane."

Thorn holstered his Colt and faced the trembling politician. "Not for me to judge," he said, "but you've got no snakes now. Maybe a short rest wouldn't do you any harm."

"I wish we'd never stopped here," Coffey said, his voice dropped almost to a whisper.

Thorn couldn't argue with the man's feelings. Instead, he left Coffey alone, scanning the shadowed corners of his room for serpents that did not exist.

ELEVEN

While Thorn had found nothing amiss in Julius Coffey's room, he spent five minutes checking out his own after he'd locked the door behind him. He checked everywhere that he could think of and found nothing more disturbing than a small beetle of some kind underneath the dresser, which he liberated through the window, wings abuzz as it took flight across Main Street. Whatever Coffey had observed, or *thought* he'd seen, the vanished rattlesnakes had not escaped to Thorn's room as a secondary hiding place.

What was it all about? He'd smelled no liquor on the politician's breath when they were standing close together, and there'd been no reek of it around his room. Imaginary snakes, in Thorn's experience, were normally a consequence of delirium tremens, suffered by drunkards on withdrawal from their alcoholic beverage of choice after prolonged intoxication. The only other explanation he could think of was insanity, but nothing he'd observed in Coffey during prior encounters—though their contact had admittedly been brief—suggested any kind of mental illness plaguing him.

A third possibility, so remote as to be dismissed out of hand, was that the Providence Hotel harbored a real-life nest of rattlers, denning as they sometimes did together, which had found an outlet into Coffey's room somehow, then managed to escape while he was clamoring for help, before Thorn's entry to the scene. That possibility seemed so unlikely that it almost made Thorn laugh.

Almost.

The fear in Coffey's eyes, on his distorted face, had been too genuine for the performance of a foolish prank, conducted without knowing whether anyone would hear his cries and answer them. He had been terrified of *something,* and if not the vipers he professed were swarming in his rented room, then what?

That stumped Thorn as he took his gunbelt off, removed his boots, and lay down for a nap before the ceremony started at sundown. He had no clue how long or late the festival would run, and while he should be free to leave at any time, if it was entertaining and he chose to stay awhile, he would be sacrificing sleep before he said good-bye to Lazarus tomorrow morning. Dozing now, if only for a half-hour or so, would help him stay awake later and do his part—whatever that might be—to celebrate the small town's anniversary as one of nine invited guests.

Thorn had a talent when it came to sleeping. His surroundings were irrelevant, whether a suite at some lavish hotel or camped on stony ground beside a crackling fire, when he had set his mind on passing from the conscious world and into sleep. Most times, if he was not preoccupied with racing thoughts, it took him five minutes or less separate himself from waking life. At the same time, his mind remained alert enough to wake, fully alert, at any slightest sound or other threatening disturbance close at hand.

Today, there was no subtlety about the sounds that roused him from a dream barely begun. The first noise was a clamoring of footsteps running down the corridor outside his room, in the direction of the hallway. Sixty seconds later, more or less, he heard a man's voice shouting in the street below his window, crying out in fear, beseeching anyone who might hear him for aid.

Thorn rose and stood before his window, looking down on Main Street. He was startled by the sight of Julius Coffee —now in shirtsleeves, barefoot after taking off his boots— running across the wooden sidewalk, out into the street, arms flailing as he cried for with force enough to strain his throat.

"They're after me!" the politician wailed. "Oh someone, please! Help me!"

Coffey had started to relax a little, still humiliated by the scene he'd made with Thorn, when they had checked his room and found no rattlers oozing from beneath his furniture or out of dresser drawers. He was a stranger to hallucinations, having never suffered one before, and he'd drunk nothing stronger than black coffee since arriving in the town of Lazarus.

How to explain the terrifying fantasy? Coffey was deeply troubled now, recalling a "peculiar" uncle on his mother's side who used to argue with the voices in his head before he'd run away from home one night and wound up drowning in a creek, the water barely deep enough for minnows to survive. Madness could run in families, he'd heard, and while the thought had never crossed his mind before, what else but sheer insanity explained the episode?

From that notion sprang abject fear of ridicule, humiliation, and expulsion from the Kansas legislature if his fellow representatives observed him raving like a lunatic out of control. The voters of his district had selected him because he was clear-headed and conservative. His backers in the shadows had invested in his new career with plans to be rewarded, sometime in the not-so-distant future. All of that would fall away if he went mad and found himself committed to the Topeka State Hospital, constructed after Osawatomie's facility was filled up to capacity.

Perhaps he only needed sleep. Granted, he'd had a full night's rest after the mental trauma of the highway robbery on Friday, blazing guns and all, but might this be some kind of curious delayed reaction to his brush with death? That thought consoled him as he kicked his boots off, slipped out of his tie and jacket, reaching out to hang them in the chifforobe—

And then recoiled as two fat rattlers tumbled from the cabinet, twining around his feet.

Coffey leaped backward, too surprised to scream. The snakes hissed at him, but they had not struck him yet. He lurched away from them, half turning toward the door, and saw at least a dozen other serpents piled up on his bed, a heap of hissing, rattling death.

He reached the door, nearly forgot that it was locked, then bolted out into the corridor, along its strip of carpet to the stairs. He nearly stumbled, going down, but caught himself and made it to the lobby, saw the clerk regarding him in shock as Coffey found his voice. He burst onto the sidewalk and across it, loose dirt underfoot, screaming, "They're after me! Oh someone, please! Help me!"

A strong male voice replied, "What seems to be the problem here?"

Coffey immediately recognized the marshal, though the lawman's name eluded him. He focused on the star pinned to the tall man's vest and babbled out, "Snakes! Rattlers! In my room upstairs! They're everywhere!"

"Snakes in the Providence?" the marshal asked. "I tend to doubt that, Mr...Coffey, is it?"

"What? Yes! And I'm telling you, I saw them. *Twice!*"

"I see." The marshal looked around them, at the townspeople who'd gathered in response to Coffey's cries. It seemed to Coffey that the marshal smiled—and were some of the others actually smiling back at him? How could they?

"We should take this off the street," the marshal said. "You're starting to upset a lot of folks."

"But—"

"Never mind, now. You just come along with me, all nice and quiet like. We'll talk about it in my office."

"No!" Coffey jerked backward from the hand that gripped his elbow. "I know what I saw! I'm not insane!"

The marshal's fist came out of nowhere, slammed into his jaw, and everything went black.

Dempsey Poppert heard somebody hollering on Main Street, but he didn't recognize the high-pitched voice. Turning in that direction as he crossed the thoroughfare, he saw some people gathered on the sidewalk outside the hotel, watching the marshal huddled with the screamer, trying to restrain him, then delivering a haymaker that put him down when all else failed.

Some lunatic, thought Poppert, as he went about his

business, moving toward the doctor's office for a second try at checking in on Warren Mapes. If his companion from the coach was still unconscious and the doctor had no explanation for it...then, what? They were scheduled for departure in the morning, if the blacksmith got their axle fixed, and there was no way he could drive with Warren slumped down on the seat beside him, likely to go flying the first time they hit a curve in the roadway. Likewise, six passengers meant there was no room for the injured shotgun guard to ride inside the coach. Strapping him atop the roof or packing him in with the luggage, in the boot, was unacceptable.

The only choice, if Warren couldn't travel, would be leaving him behind until he healed—and what would happen then? Who would come back and fetch him, pay the doctor's bill, and see to Warren's ultimate recovery when he was clear of Lazarus? The trips they'd made together, all the times they'd talked of nothing in particular, Poppert had no idea where Warren Mapes called home. For all he knew, the guard was constantly in transit, sleeping over nights at this or that station and waiting for another day out on the trail, protecting strangers and their goods.

But if he couldn't work, what would become of him?

Barlow & Sanderson had no retirement plan for its employees, no pension, and damn sure no home set aside for drivers or their guards who passed beyond the time when they were any service to the company. A young man started working for the coach line, and he left its employ as an old man if he lived that long, to look out for himself during the time that he had left.

So what? It was the same as any other job that Poppert knew of. At the moment, he was focusing on here and now, Mapes sleeping like a mummy at the doctor's office, with the sawbones claiming that he didn't have a clue about the cause.

Poppert's agitation was reflected in his knocking on the doctor's door. It took a while, like last time, for the medic to appear and frown at him. Before he even got a word out, Dr. Horn announced, "I am afraid there's been no change."

"Nothin' at all?"

"I'm sorry, no." He didn't *sound* sorry, but Poppert chalked that up to his own nerves.

"Okay. That sedative you give him?"

"Yes?"

"Have you got somethin' in your office there, some kinda medicine that would reverse it? Wake him up, whether he's done sleepin' or not?"

"You have to understand the danger if I—"

"Look, Doc! All I know is that my pard come to you with his shoulder hurt, and now he's in some kinda coma, whatever you fellas call it. That sounds wrong to me, and if your medicine's what tipped him over, then it's up to you to bring him back!"

"My dear sir—"

"Don't 'dear sir' me, Doc. Warren's my friend, and what I see, you carin' for him's made him go from bad to worse."

The doctor frowned at him, same old expression, then nodded and said, "Please, come inside."

Poppert brushed past him, heard the door close, and was moving toward the room where Mapes slept when a hand clutching a rag that smelled like bitter medicine was clamped over his nose and mouth. The doctor's other arm locked tight across his chest. Poppert struggled, tried reaching for his holstered Colt, but he could feel his strength deserting him.

Another moment, and the room tilted, then faded out to black.

Thorn watched from his hotel window as Marshal Farrell cold-cocked Julius Coffey, caught him on the fall, and hoisted him over one shoulder, moving off beneath his dead weight toward the lawman's office, on the far side of Main Street. Below, the crowd of watchers dissipated, several of them smiling, talking animatedly among themselves.

Thorn had no idea what had transpired between the marshal and the shouting, agitated politician once they met up on the thoroughfare. He guessed it was a good thing Farrell was nearby, rather than letting Coffey run for any distance, screaming about phantom rattlesnakes in his hotel room. Thorn had seen Farrell reach out for Coffey, saw the lawmaker pull back and say something that didn't reach his ears upstairs, through panes of glass, and then the marshal had employed one punch to take the fight out of what seemed to be a madman raving on the thoroughfare.

Better than pulling out a gun and grappling for it, maybe shooting Coffey dead.

But what had caused the second fit of Coffey's strange reptilian hallucinations, when he'd seen, with Thorn, that there was nothing lurking in his hotel room?

Away down Main Street, Thorn saw Dempsey Poppert crossing toward the doctor's office while the marshal carried Coffey out of sight behind his labeled door. Poppert knocked on the medic's door and waited for an answer, then palavered with the doctor for a while before he disappeared inside, the door closing behind him.

Checking on his friend, no doubt, and why did that make Thorn uneasy, when he turned his mind to it? He thought of Warren Mapes, the shotgun guard, whose dislocated shoulder would have benefited from a sling, but which did not—at least in Thorn's opinion—call for any manner of extended supervision. It was well beyond a day now, since his fall, and he had not emerged form Dr. Hornaby's establishment as yet.

Peculiar? Couple that with Julius Coffey's serpentine hallucinations and the screams that Laurel Dycus had reported, shattering her first night's sleep in Lazarus, and had some kind of pattern started to emerge? Was something happening in town, bizarre enough to presage danger for the stagecoach passengers, yet still obscure to Thorn's focused imagination?

And if so, more to the point, what could he do about it now, before the festival began at dusk?

Nothing but stay alert and ready for whatever happened next.

Laurel Dycus woke from troubled dreams of being chased through darkness by unseen pursuers when the church bell started chiming over Lazarus. She rose from bed, moved toward her window facing Main Street, and saw townspeople emerging from their shops or habitations in the fading light of dusk, all moving toward the church in something close to lockstep, little conversation shared among them as they passed.

Time for the festival, she thought, mildly surprised to find that she was dreading it.

Her time in Lazarus so far had not been restful. While

there'd been no repetition of the screams she'd heard on Friday night, that incident had soured her on lingering around the town, and no talk of the anniversary extravaganza was about to change her mind. Something was *off* about the whole damned town, and while she couldn't put her finger on it—from the smiles of strangers that seemed artificial, to the sickly smell of flowers on display outside their stores—she simply knew something was *wrong*.

In short, it had the feeling of a town where strangers passing through would normally be shunned, discouraged from remaining any longer than it took to buy supplies and move along, rather than being honored, feted at a celebration of the settlement's atrocious past. Perhaps that was the sour note that troubled Laurel, urging her to skip the ceremony, double-lock her door, and stay completely out of sight.

Against that feeling was her lifelong attitude, refusing to be cowed by anyone or anything.

She had undressed for bed, down to her underwear, upon returning to her room that afternoon. Now, she put on a dress the locals had not seen before, laced up her shoes, and donned a feathered hat she held in place with hairpins. She studied herself in the mirror and found nothing out of place, not up to snuff for welcoming a first-rate brothel's customers, but good enough for Lazarus and its anniversary of a war crime.

Laurel didn't plan to take the town by storm. She would be satisfied to mingle with her fellow stagecoach passengers, accept whatever praise or small award was set aside for them as "honored" guests, and move along tomorrow while she put the place out of her mind for good. This was an episode in her ongoing life and nothing more.

So, why was she so apprehensive as she peered around the hotel room for anything she might have overlooked?

Her weapons.

Moving swiftly to her bag, she removed the Colt Open Top Pocket Model Revolver checked its load, and slipped it down into a hidden pocket sewn into her skirt for that specific purpose. The pearl-handled switchblade disappeared inside Laurel's left sleeve, secured there by a piece of elastic that held it in place, out of sight, till she gave it a yank, pressed its button, and went for an enemy's eyes, face, or throat.

Surprise!

The odds were long against her needing either knife or gun this evening, but she felt better now that she was armed, almost as if she'd nearly left the room without her hat, or something even more important, like her blouse. She would no sooner walk the length of Main Street naked than she would attend the festival unarmed.

Now she was prepared. Let the festivities begin.

TWELVE

It didn't happen often—next to never, if the truth be told—but on that waning afternoon of Saturday the twenty-fifth, Thorn heard a simultaneous alarm from Storm and Bell, down at the livery. He recognized their psychic voices instantly, from their exchanges of ideas on countless winding trails. Their message, urgent and arresting, used no words, but still impressed him with the need to drop what he was doing, grab his Winchester and Sharps, and hurry to the stable, two blocks from the Providence Hotel. It also warned him to avoid as many human beings as he could along the way.

Thorn slipped out through the hotel's backdoor, circumventing any contact with a watchful clerk positioned in the lobby. He had no idea of what was wrong as yet, but steeled himself against the possibility of injury to one or both of his domestic creatures. In which case, if it were true, someone would pay a price.

No one observed him as he ran along behind the Main Street shops and came up on the livery's blind side. A door for people stood beside the larger double door for horses, and it was not locked. Thorn slipped inside, emitting all the soothing energy that he could manage, as he had since fleeing from the Providence Hotel. Both animals seemed calmer now, no signals indicating pain from physical assault, relieved that Thorn had come to them so quickly, but an undertone of worry still remained.

They wanted out, that much was obvious, and Thorn thought, *What the hell. Why not?*

The hostler had offered him free board upon arrival, but he'd paid the standard one-night rate regardless, and by leaving now, he ought to skip the second night while cheating no one. Setting down his rifles in a corner of the stallion's stall, he spoke to Shadow first, then called on Bell and stroked her neck until her general demeanor seemed serene, though she still trembled slightly while she broadcast thoughts of fear.

Get on with it.

He saddled Shadow first, less time-consuming than the process with his mule, then doubled back and started hoisting packs onto the padded frame Bell wore when they were traveling. Thorn had the last bundle in place, when suddenly a voice spoke up behind him, almost touching-close.

"You can't leave yet," it said.

He turned to face a burly, bearded man he didn't recognize from Friday, face smudged by a blacksmith's labors, stomach bulging at a leather apron meant to spare his clothes from sparks and red-hot coals.

"Can't help it, friend," Thorn said. "I'm in a hurry, as you see. I paid up for last night, but if you need another fifty cents—"

"You can't run off before the festival," the stranger said, and smiled with crooked, yellow teeth.

"I'll try to catch it next year," Thorn replied. "For now, though—"

"You. Can't. Go."

"Says who?"

The big man glanced around, then smiled again. "I do."

Thorn knew his skills and limitations. He had studied martial arts of Africa under Obi Magoro and had grown proficient in their use. He walked up to the hostler, smiling, emanating friendliness, and then launched a flurry of concerted blows against his shaggy face.

Which seemed to pass through air, without effect.

The hostler laughed, gripped Thorn by his lapels, and tossed him like a rag doll from Bell's stall, against a stack of hay bales ranged along the wall. Thorn scrambled to his feet, retreating toward the blacksmith's forge, still loathe to use his pistols on an unarmed man, trying to make sense of his inability to strike the man.

It made no sense at all, unless...

A legend came to Thorn unbidden, and he bolted toward the forge, looking for something that could serve him as a weapon if his dark suspicion was correct. He found it in a cast-iron poker, clutched the rod with its barbed tip, and turned to swing it just as his assailant rushed to close the gap between them, snarling.

Where his fists had failed a moment earlier, the blackened poker seemed to *split* the hostler open from his scalp to groin, dividing him in two, but where a normal man should have been spilling entrails, this one—not a man, by any means—*exploded* into dust like talcum powder settling in a cloud onto the stable's floor.

Thorn had run out of time for pondering the strange

event. He fetched Bell from her stall and mounted Shadow, then risked riding through the livery's front doors, despite the threat of being seen. Once clear, he poured on speed and didn't stop until they were well out of Lazarus.

Dempsey Poppert woke, trussed up like a Thanksgiving turkey ready for the oven, in a backroom of the doctor's office. Warren Mapes, still snoring softly in his drug-induced unconsciousness, lay on a second cot nearby. Poppert still smelled and tasted the revolting chloroform that Dr. Hornaby had used to overwhelm him, and he knew at once his gunbelt had been stripped from him while he was lying helpless and inert.

What in the goddamned hell was going on?

He didn't have a clue, but realized that Hornaby had lied to him from the beginning, about Warren's shoulder, about everything. Hornaby always meant to hold the shotgun rider prisoner, and now Poppert had played into his hands as well, a fact that made him feel a perfect idiot.

Nobody's perfect, said a small voice in his mind, and Poppert nearly laughed at that, before a coughing fit took over and he rolled onto his side, to keep a batch of phlegm from choking him.

"Ah, you're awake," the doctor said from somewhere off behind him, sounding pleased. "I'm glad. You should appreciate the ceremony, after all. I'll rouse your partner in a moment, then the others can collect you."

"C'lect us why? What for?" Poppert demanded, conscious that his words were somewhat slurred from the sedation.

"For the festival, of course," said Dr. Hornaby, now stepping into Poppert's field of vision, bending over Warren's cot. "You won't be sleeping through it. Heavens no! You'll have the full experience."

"I'd just as soon skip that," said Poppert.

"Nonsense. It's the honor of a lifetime, serving others, even if that wasn't your intention when you hobbled into Lazarus."

"The others?"

"They will all be reunited, never fear. It shall be glorious for all or you. For all of *us*."

Hornaby passed what Poppert took for smelling salts under his partner's nose and Warren spluttered back to life, demanding to know what was happening. Before Hornaby had a chance to answer, Mapes saw Poppert on his own low cot and cried out, "Dempsey? What in hell?"

"Looks like a buncha crazy people have us," Poppert answered.

"Crazy?" Dr. Hornaby couldn't resist a laugh at that. "You're in for a surprise, my friends. A very *great* surprise, indeed."

Julius Coffey heard somebody walking through the marshal's office, heavy footsteps drawing nearer by the second. Moving to the wall of bars that formed the front side of his cell, he saw the marshal—Farrell, was it?— watching him with an inquisitive expression on his face.

"I'm better now," he said, before the lawman had an opportunity to speak. "I understand why you were worried earlier, excited as I was and being loud, but I'm a city boy at heart, you understand. Those snakes, inside my hotel room...it was a shock, you know?"

"All over that?" the marshal asked. "Able to walk and talk like anybody else, without a lot of fuss?"

"Yes! Absolutely right!"

"I hope that's true. I'd hate to have you turn up for the ceremony wearing manacles and shackles, Mr. Coffey."

"Ceremony?" Coffey's mind was blank for ten or fifteen seconds, then he said, "Oh, yes! The *ceremony*. I remember now, but in the circumstances, I thought—"

"You have been invited," Farrell told him. "You'll participate."

"Well, shouldn't I at least clean up a little, first? Change clothes, perhaps, assuming that you got those filthy snakes out of my room, and—"

"You'll be fine, just as you are," the marshal said. "I promise you. No fancy dress required, although most of the townsfolk wear their Sunday best."

"I'd hate to disappoint them, Marshal, looking shabby as I do right now. If I could just—"

Farrell produced a key, moved closer, saying, "When I open up your cell, you have two choices. Come along with me, all peaceful like, or I will shoot you in the knee and carry you. That hurts like hell, in case you couldn't guess."

Stunned into blinking silence, Coffey stared at Farrell for the better part of half a minute, then replied, "I'll come along, of course."

"Good man. It's better when you show up under your own power, voluntarily. No screaming and carrying on at the start, don't you see?"

At the start? Coffey watched as his cell was unlocked, the door opened, willing his legs to respond with a single step forward, but they seemed divorced from his brain. What did Farrell mean, no screaming *at the start?*

He found his voice, a whisper of its normal self, and asked, "There will be screaming then? Later?"

"Oh, I expect so, yes," the marshal said. "It's pretty much traditional. Cries of delight from us, the spawn of Lazarus. Perhaps a somewhat different noise from our invited guests."

Coffey's legs buckled then, and would have dropped him to the floor if Farrell hadn't rushed inside the cell to catch him, hold him more or less erect with one arm wrapped tightly around the politician's shoulders. A second later, Coffey heard the *click-clack* of a pistol being cocked. He glanced downward and saw a six-gun in the marshal's right hand, muzzle hovering mere inches from his knee.

"Time for a firm decision, Mr. Coffey," Farrell said. "Will you be walking to the festival, or does the pain start now?"

"I'm coming!" Coffey blurted out. "I just...don't understand."

"That's fine," Farrell replied. "You will. You will."

"I find this *very* tiresome, Eldridge," Florence Mottinger declared—not for the first time and, her husband would have bet, not for the last.

"We've been invited," he reminded her. "After the town's supplied free room and board, it is the very least that we can do."

"So you keep saying," she responded, as they cleared the hotel lobby, stepping out onto Main Street at dusk. "And don't you find it *tres* peculiar, everything that's happened since we landed here?"

She was pretending to be French again, using one of the few words that she'd memorized and managing to mispronounce it "tress." Eldridge was thankful they had never gone to France, despite Flo's nagging at him through the years. He made his mind up then and there, they never would.

"I see nothing peculiar," he replied. "A town preparing for its revels on an anniversary takes pity on a group of stranded travelers. Christians might call them Good Samaritans."

Flo made a little clucking sound and said, "It isn't right, if you ask me."

He longed to say *I didn't and I wouldn't,* but the argument that would inevitably follow put him off. Instead, he told his wife, "Stiff upper lip. Let's see it through and hope to get away from here tomorrow morning, eh?"

"Please God!" she fairly moaned.

As if summoned, three men stepped from an alleyway, blocking their progress toward the church, its bell still tolling on monotonously. Eldridge recognized two of them as the brothers who had earlier accosted Florence and himself, accompanied this evening by a rangy third man whom he hadn't seen before.

"We meet again," one of the brothers said. "Surprise!"

"Surprise!" the other sibling echoed, grinning like a cretin.

Eldridge glanced along Main Street—no sign of Marshal Farrell anywhere—before he said, "We're going to the festival. Please stand aside and let us pass."

"We'll do better 'n that," the third man said. "Gonna escort you down there, like the king and queen you think you are."

"Some king," the older of the brothers smirked. "Some queen."

"Now listen here!" Florence began, then ended with a

meek, strangled "Oh, my," as Older Brother pulled a pocket pistol from beneath his baggy shirt ant cocked it.

"Go ahead, Queenie," he smirked at her. "What'd you wanna say?"

"Um, nothing," Flo replied, the meekest Eldridge could remember hearing from her in his life. "Nothing at all."

"Tha's what I thought," the gunman said. "Now, you two walk ahead of us, all nice and proper like. No trouble, and there'll be no bleedin' any sooner than there has to be."

Alarmed by that, Eldridge said, "Marshal Farrell won't be pleased with you for this."

"Give us a job to do," the third man said. "We's doin' it."

"A job?" Eldridge could not help asking."

"Bring you to the festival, like it or not."

"But we were on our way, before you stopped us," Flo protested in a shaky voice.

"Can't take no chances on the anniversary," the gunman said, as if that answered everything.

"This anniversary of yours," Eldridge began.

"You're gonna love it," Older Brother said. "You'll be the center of attention, like you always wanna be. Well, you and those that come in with you yesterday."

"But I don't understand," Eldridge replied.

"Don't need to, yet. You *will*, though. And you *will* be sorry. Bet your life on that."

Thorn stubbornly resisted the idea that filled his mind, but he could not defeat it. While it was outlandish, he saw no other solution that encompassed all the facts.

The hostler he had grappled with had been a ghost.

All of the details added up, from his fists punching

through the stranger's face and head, to cast-iron finally destroying him. Thorn had not been hallucinating, had not dreamed the battle, and with that in mind, he gave another thought to Julius Coffey and the rattlers he had seen inside his hotel room.

Specters? Why not? Thorn's personal belief system, such as it was, accepted that the animals around him all had souls—and if that supposition was correct, why shouldn't they pass on?

The only question that remained: why would a spectral blacksmith try to stop him slipping out of Lazarus before the celebration of its anniversary?

The answer struck Thorn like a right hook to his gut. Of course, it *wasn't* just the stable keeper. Not only the barber who had pressed a razor to his throat that morning. Not only the drunks who had harassed the Mottingers. Not only Marshal Farrell or the minister who dressed them down for it—the selfsame minister who showed up at the barber-shop, perhaps in time to save Thorn's life.

It was the whole damned town.

Shadow and Bell were both greatly relieved to have the place behind them, but Thorn's mind was buzzing now. How could this happen? What did it portend?

The first question was simply answered, once the concept of surviving spirits was accepted. Sudden, violent death more commonly produced a haunting than when people slipped beyond the veil from natural disease, or in their sleep. Thorn's reading on the subject told him that a murder or a suicide often left business still unfinished on the Earthly plane: a craving for revenge, perhaps, or simple closure to a life cut short. And Lazarus, pillaged by Bloody Bill's guerrillas on this very date, eleven years ago, was ripe for cultivating hostile shades.

The town had never been rebuilt, he guessed, never reoccupied. If Thorn was right, it simply *rose* upon the anniversary of its destruction, former residents going about their business as they had in life, eager to fasten on whatever living souls might pass through Lazarus on the appointed day.

Why now, in the eleventh year, instead of more auspicious anniversaries—the tenth, the twentieth, and so on? Never mind. For all Thorn knew, the ghost town rose from nothing *every* year, and would continue doing so until its spectral residents were laid to rest.

As for the ceremony's "honored guests," he had no doubt that they would be consumed.

Thorn reined his stallion in and murmured soft encouragement, to Shadow and to Bell. They'd come perhaps a mile from Lazarus, and it was darker now. If he was going to return, to *do* something—whatever that might be—he'd have to hurry now.

He left Shadow and Bell standing beside a copse of desert willows and mescal, with water rising from around their roots, stripping them of their travel gear. He told them, audibly, "I'll come back here as soon as possible. It may be dawn or later. If I don't return by noon, come back to town. It should be safe by then."

For animals, at least.

Toting his Winchester, leaving the long-range Sharps behind, Thorn started back toward Lazarus on foot. He had a mile in which to rehash what he knew of ghosts—and, more specifically, about disposing of them. Iron worked, obviously, but he couldn't very well take on the town's whole spectral population with a blacksmith's poker. They would overwhelm him and...well, he had no idea what happened after that.

It hit him when he was a quarter mile from Lazarus, at least a partial answer to his problem, though it posed some difficulties of its own. First, he would have to find the coach gun from the stage, together with its ammunition belt, then he would need a decent quantity of salt.

Above all else, he hoped he'd be in time to help the coach's passengers and crew.

THIRTEEN

When Laurel Dycus left the Providence Hotel there was no clerk on duty at the registration desk. The church bell kept on clamoring outside, and she supposed the man had left his post to witness the ensuing big event, whatever that entailed. There was a crowd outside the church, members lined up to make their way inside, prompting her to consider whether they would all fit in the pews.

She was considering a turnaround, returning to her room, when she saw Marshal Farrell come out of his office, leading Julius Coffey after him, keeping a firm grip on the politician's arm. Coffey was arguing, face twisted up in fear, perhaps in anger, as he kept pace with the lawman. Laurel couldn't hear what he was saying, but Farrell seemed deaf to it, propelling Coffey down the wooden sidewalk, toward the church.

They'd covered half a block when Coffey tried to break away and Laurel saw his wrists were manacled. Before he could escape, Farrell lashed out and punched him in the face, slamming him up against the front wall of a shop. Laurel ducked back into the hotel's doorway, out of sight, just as the marshal turned to sweep Main Street with narrowed eyes.

Now what in hell...?

The ugly scene made up her mind: she absolutely was not going to the church for any kind of ceremony, "honored guest" or not. Laurel stepped back into the lobby, half turned toward the staircase, then she realized her upstairs room would be the first place anybody looked for her when they discovered she was missing from the festival. Checking the street again, she saw Farrell retreating with his prisoner and ducked out quickly, darting toward an alley on her left.

Now, where to go?

She thought about the livery. If there was no one there to stop her, she could steal a horse, perhaps even a buggy, and get out of Lazarus before she was discovered and restrained. Horse theft might get her hanged if she were caught—she wasn't well versed on the laws in Kansas—but she liked her chances running better than she liked them staying put.

Ducking around behind the Providence Hotel, she started for the livery and nearly made it. She was still a half block short, however, when three men who looked like death warmed over popped out of another passageway between two Main Street shops and barred her path.

"Can't have you runnin' off now, Missy," one of them declared.

"Won't do at all," another added, while the third stood mute.

"I'm late for an appointment at the livery," she said. "Now, if you'll step aside—"

"You're late, awright," the first one cut her off. "They's waitin' for you at the festival."

As frightened as she was, Laurel knew what to do. She

wasted no more time on words, but yanked the switchblade from her sleeve and snapped it open, going for the speaker's throat. The long stiletto blade was right on target, but it passed through without loosing the expected tide of blood. Laurel felt nothing but a very slight resistance, as if she had sliced a dangling piece of silk.

The man whose throat she should have slashed was laughing in her face.

"You gotta do better than that, you feisty bitch!" he said.

"How's this?" a voice asked from behind the trio, and she saw Gideon Thorn attacking with some object like a fireplace poker, flailing left and right. Each time he struck one of the strangers with his blackened club, the man on the receiving end burst into dusty fragments, settling toward the ground. The last one shattered managed to unleash a windy, high-pitched wail before he fell apart.

"Are you all right?" Thorn asked her, stepping close.

She backed up half a pace from him, gaping, snapping out, "I sure as hell *am not?* What were those things?"

"You'd likely call them ghosts," he said, matter-of-factly. "We can talk about that later. Will you help me fight the rest of them and save your friends?"

"You mean the others from the stage? They're not my friends, but yes. I'll help you if I can."

"It means a fight, likely with everybody else in town," he said.

"We won't get far with that," she told him, nodding toward the poker in his hand. "Why not just use your guns?"

"The bullets wouldn't work on this crowd. Iron's all right, but what we need for them in bunches would be salt."

Fearing the young man might have lost his mind, she echoed, "Salt?"

Nodding, Thorn said, "I figure we can get it from the restaurant. But first, I need the coach gun from the stage and any extra shells the guard was carrying."

Deciding not to argue, she replied, "We'd better check the coach then, hadn't we?

"My brethren and my sisters!" Standing at the lectern in his chapel, Hezekiah Gates spoke forcefully to make his deep voice audible in every pew, over the murmuring of the assembled celebrants. They slowly settled down, eyes turning toward the dais, riveted by Gates.

"The moment we have waited for is drawing closer," he reminded them unnecessarily. "All year we languish, and the time will soon be ripe. Bring forward our assembled guests and let them each be recognized."

Below, he saw Doc Hornaby and two assistants bringing up the coach crew members. Three others tussled briefly with an older couple from the stage, while Marshal Farrell brought a well-dressed but disheveled man in manacles.

"We have a problem, Pastor," Farrell said, his voice nearly as loud as Gate's. "We're missing four of them of them so far. Three passengers and Thorn, the young fella who followed them to town."

"Four out of nine?" Gates felt his rage mounting. "That's nearly half! It is completely unacceptable. Besides which, who knows what they're doing if they are not here among us?"

"We can find them," Farrell said. "There's no place they can hide from us in Lazarus."

"And yet, you've lost them!" Gates roared back at him. "This must be rectified *immediately!* Leave a few guards here, for those you managed to collect, and *find the rest! Go now!*"

They rose as one, babbling, swept from the sanctuary on the hot wave of his wrath. A handful lingered, cringing from him, gathering around the five terrified prisoners. Addressing those who'd stayed behind, Gates growled, "Stay here until the rest of us return. Do not move from this spot, come Hell or Judgment Day. You understand?"

Their heads bobbed silently, prepared to follow any order that he handed down as if it were the very word of God. Descending from his pulpit, Gates swept past them, stalked along the aisle dividing pews inside his church, and passed through open doors into a night gone suddenly, infuriatingly awry.

Delbert Akins had planned to have a drink or three before the festival. Most parties, he'd have counted on some free booze flowing, but it seemed the folks in Lazarus were bent on celebrating in a church, which didn't bode well for a quenching of his thirst. The Glory Hole was open, though, or seemed to be, light streaming from its windows and around its batwing doors into the long shadows of prairie dusk.

If there were any other drinkers in the place, who knew? He might even be able to squeeze in a game of cards, gambling the pittance he had left after his humbling loss on Friday night.

Akins glanced toward the church as he was crossing Main Street from the Providence Hotel. The steeple bell had ended its infernal clanging, sweet relief, and he supposed most of the townsfolk—maybe all of them—were packed inside the chapel, with its doors shut now against impending darkness.

Banners on the street, hailing the anniversary of whatever it was, hung limp without a breeze to stir them. Up and down Main Street, by lamplight, Akins saw bouquets of flowers, looking strangely wilted now, and ribbons dangling slack outside of storefront entrances. A man inclined toward thinking beyond cards and dice, liquor and easy women, might have said that Lazarus looked dead.

Akins shoved through the Glory Hole's twin swinging doors, a squeal of rusty hinges that he hadn't noticed last night grating on his nerves. He mouthed a curse at finding the place empty, though its lamps were lit and glowing, no sign of a human being anywhere in sight.

"Hello!" he called out to the emptiness. "Is anybody home?"

A sudden thought occurred to him. He shouted toward the bar and up beyond it, to the second floor, "Any objections if I take a couple bottles for the road, and maybe have a beer or two? I guess it's on the house tonight?"

When no one answered, he moved toward the bar, and then around behind it, reaching for two bottles of the best and most expensive whiskey he could find. Setting the bottles on the bar, Akins picked up a mug and started filling it with beer on tap.

He was about to sip the brew and let its head give him a white mustache, when something flickered at the corner of his eye. Turning in that direction, toward the far end of the bar, he saw a tall man in an apron over shirtsleeves, standing where he hadn't been a second earlier.

The bartender from nowhere turned to Akins, smiled with crooked yellow teeth, and said, "Straggler."

Akins had no idea what that meant, but he had been caught red-handed. Lying as he always did when facts were all against him, he said, "Look, this isn't what it seems..."

Before he could say more, another voice, this one behind him, muttered, "Straggler."

Akins spun to face a shorter, rounder man, whose overall appearance was no better than the flighty bartender's. They came at him together, arms outstretched, both grinning vacuously. Akins dropped his beer mug to the floor, soaking his trouser cuffs, and drew the derringer from his vest pocket, cocking it. He aimed first at the barkeep, who advanced with no reaction, then off toward the shorter man, who actually laughed.

"I'll shoot!" Akins advised. "Don't think I won't!"

"It won't help you," the shorter man proclaimed, and rushed headlong at him.

"Shouldn't the coach be at the livery?" Laurel Dycus asked, as she followed Thorn in the opposite direction.

"Should be," Thorn replied. "It's not, though. Just four horses from the team, together with their harness."

"So, the blacksmith wasn't really working on it?"

"No. The whole town's played you all for fools. Me too, and *I* should know better."

When he didn't explain the last remark, Laurel asked him, "What was that you said about these...*ghosts*...and salt?"

"You saw how iron works on them," Thorn replied. "According to some texts, salt does the same. Direct contact supposedly can dissipate a ghost."

"Supposedly?"

He shrugged. "We won't know till we try."

"And what about the coach gun?"

"It's a shotgun. I can open up the shells, pack them with salt, and use a bit of cloth to keep it in each one. If I get close enough, it ought to take them down. Or not."

"Think, positive, for God's sake! Now, this shotgun. Where is it?"

"Unless the marshal took it," Thorn replied, it should be with the coach."

"But not down art the livery."

Thorn shook his head emphatically. "First place I looked."

"And what about your animals? The horse and mule?"

"They're safe for now," he said.

"You took them out ahead of anybody else? Well, thanks for coming back for me, I think."

"I didn't," Thorn informed her. I just figured, if they tried to stash the coach where none of us would spot it, it must be behind the shops, one side of Main Street or the other. I picked east to start and there you were."

"So, just coincidence?"

"Unless you want to call it Fate. Come on. Let's check behind the west side shops. It won't be long until they're looking for us."

"They already have the Mottingers, the politician, and the stagecoach crew," she told him, as they moved along an alley toward the thoroughfare.

"I saw the marshal taking Julius Coffey," Thorn replied. "Now hush!"

They'd reached the alley's mouth and hesitated there. Thorn peered from cover, up and down the street, spotting no danger straightaway.

"All right, come on!"

He bolted, heard her skirt and petticoats swishing behind him as she tried to match his loping pace. Reaching another alley opposite the one they'd come from, Thorn led her behind the shops and offices on that side, took another hasty glance before emerging from its cover, and immediately saw the stagecoach parked behind the Glory Hole.

It was a moment's work to find the shotgun, in the footwell of the driver's seat. Apparently, ghosts had no used for firearms and had left it there. Thorn tucked it underneath his left arm, Winchester in his right hand, and looped a bandolier of cartridges over his shoulder. Laurel clutched the poker, keeping watch.

Nodding to southward, he told her, "Down there stands Adeline's. Smart money says nobody's home tonight."

They didn't have to break into the restaurant. Its backdoor was unlocked, Thorn opened it, then handed Laurel his rifle and the coach gun, taking back the poker she'd been carrying because his hands were full.

"Stick close to me," he whispered to her on the dark threshold, "but give me room to swing if someone jumps out at us."

"Understood," she said.

But he'd been right again: no one was home. They ducked into the kitchen, shielded from the dining room's windows by inner walls, and Thorn managed to light a lamp before he started searching for the salt. It only took a moment, with the light, to find a keg of salt standing beside the café's grill. Thorn put it on the floor, sat down beside it, pulled a knife and started prying up the lid as he told Laurel, "May as well be comfortable."

Dropping to the floor was awkward, in her present garb, but Laurel managed it. "Now what?" she asked.

"First thing, we have to open these," Thorn said.

Swiftly, he pulled the shotgun cartridges out of their bandolier loops rolling them across the floor to Laurel. He removed a dagger from its sheath in his right boot and demonstrated on the first one, prying at the crimping on its business end with the knife's blade. As she watched, Laura flicked open her switchblade.

"Do this to all of them," he said, as he poured out the lead pellets of buckshot from the opened shell. "The powder is behind a piece of wadding, so you don't risk spilling that. When all the shot's out, I'll refill them from the salt keg. All I need now is some cloth to plug them nice and tight."

"Table napkins?" Laurel offered.

"Just the thing," he said, and got up, moving to a corner where fresh napkins lay folded and stacked. He brought back half a dozen and began to shred them with his boot knife, while Laurel opened the other rounds and threw their shot aside.

"You haven't told me why this works on ghosts," she said.

"I'd have to study up on it," Thorn answered, "but I know that it's *supposed* to. That comes from the same books that suggested iron, and you've seen what that does to them."

"And if your books are wrong about the salt? What, then?"

"In that case," he replied, "I'm guessing that they'll either kill us outright, or we'll have to join the celebration —which I'm guessing will amount to the same thing."

"Why are they doing this?"

"I don't know what ghosts think," he told her, "though it seems they *do* think. From the things I've seen and heard, I'd say they're focused on revenge."

"For what?"

"Today's the anniversary of Lazarus being destroyed by Rebel raiders in the war. Most of the folks—the *ghosts*— we've seen and met were probably killed here, that night."

"Most?"

"There's a theory that a place of tragic history can draw ghosts in like a magnet pulls iron filings from the dirt. They answer to the draw and make themselves at home."

"Does that explain the screams I heard last night?"

"We'll likely never know," Thorn mused, "but I'd bet it explains the rattlesnakes in Mr. Coffey's room."

"The *what?*"

"Don't worry about that," he told her. "Right now, it's the least of our concerns."

FOURTEEN

Orin Pinkham missed the ceremony's start by accident. Upon awakening to find his money satchel empty, he had counted out the paltry sum remaining in his pockets, got dressed, and went off to buy the cheapest bottle of liquid oblivion the Glory Hole saloon would sell him. That accomplished, he returned to his hotel room with the whiskey, started drinking, and passed out sometime in early afternoon. A church bell's tolling woke him rudely, close to sundown, with his bladder nearly bursting, and he'd rushed downstairs, still fully dressed, to use the hotel's privy out in back.

While he was in there, alternately sighing with relief and clutching at his head, which seemed about to detonate, he heard the bell stop its incessant clamoring. Short moments later, from the general direction of Main Street, another sound demanded his attention. This time, it was human voices mixed together, sounding angry, frightened, *something*. It reminded Pinkham of a lynch mob he had witnessed as a child and set his aching teeth on edge.

Who could the mob be searching for? Why would its

members wish to harm someone on this, their sainted anniversary?

Cautiously, Pinkham stood, hitched up his pants, and poked his nose outside the privy's simple wooden door. The sound of growling voices instantly got louder, although whether they were actually drawing nearer to him, he could not have said.

Pinkham wished he had a weapon. How on Earth had he forgotten that when he was leaving Kansas City? All that money in his bag, and bounty hunters likely on his trail, but it had not occurred to him that he might need some means of self-defense.

A lot of good it would have done him, after all, when someone slipped into his room by night, purloined his stolen loot, and slipped back out again, leaving him fast asleep, oblivious. How stupid was he, really? Even when his cash was literally lifted from the circle of his arms, he did not stir, much less put up a fight.

He still puzzled over the method of the robbery—and more so over *who* had known he had the money in the first place. If a bounty hunter had retrieved it for his bank, surely they would have taken him along as well, their prisoner bound for a trial and prison cell. It made no sense, and half the fury that he felt was focused on the mystery itself.

A sharp cry from the unseen mob alerted him that some of them had changed direction. They were definitely drawing closer now, along an alleyway located north of the hotel. His time was short, and Pinkham realized he had two choices: lock himself inside the privy, hoping no one tried the door, or bolt and run like hell.

He ran.

Behind him, a male voice alerted others, "There goes one of them!" He didn't grasp the reference, but put more concentrated effort into fleeing, feeling all the while that he must soon regurgitate the liquor he'd consumed that morning. If he stopped to vomit they would have him, so he ran and puked at the same time, soiling himself and further sickened by the stench of it, so that he retched again. If he had ever been more miserable in his misspent life, Pinkham could not recall the time or place.

And when he stumbled, sprawling, it was almost a relief. Not quite, as leading members of the mob caught up with him, but any respite for his burning lungs and thigh muscles was welcome in that moment. Rough hands pinched and prodded him, then rolled him over on his back.

"By God, he's filthy!" someone said, a woman's voice.

"He'll be worse when we finish with him," a man replied, and others laughed before the same voice said, "Come on. Let's get him to the church."

Huddled in Adeline's kitchen, Gideon Thorn and Laurel Dycus heard the mob baying along Main Street, beyond the café's public dining room. Thorn hoped the windows facing on the thoroughfare would satisfy the hunters, with their clear view of an empty room, abandoned tables, and at first, he thought they'd pulled it off.

But no such luck.

After the first wave of the hunt passed by, their racket fading, Thorn was packing the reloaded shotgun shells into their bandolier, with two inserted in the coach gun's double barrels. As he closed the weapon's breech with a decisive *snap,* He heard the crack and tinkle of a window or a glass door being broken—not entirely smashed, but just enough, he thought, to let an arm slip through and open up the inside latch.

Now, he heard footsteps in the vacant dining room, and voices whispering.

He slung the bandolier over his head and gave the blacksmith's poker back to Laurel, silently mouthing the message, *Follow me.* He blew the lamp out, wondering if it had already betrayed them to the restaurant's invaders, even though they shouldn't have observed it, but who really knew what ghosts could see or how the living world appeared to them?

Thorn stood, with Laurel rising up a second later, shifting her position so that he would face the kitchen's first intruders. No one spoke a word beyond the kitchen doorway now, but their footsteps were clearly audible, advancing toward the room where Adeline's had once prepared delicious food.

Ghost food? Thorn asked himself, and felt his stomach clench a little.

Half turning from the unseen enemy, he whispered back at Laurel, "Have you heard a shotgun fire up close, before?"

She nodded, clutched the poker in both hands as if she were a player in one of those odd, time-wasting baseball games she'd read about in newspapers. Whether Thorn's shotgun shells would work or not, but she had *seen* the poker strike down hostile spirits and she trusted it.

Could ghosts be killed, when they were already deceased? Again, Laurel didn't know, but from the dusty piles of ash-like substance that remained after they blew apart, she thought they must be *changed,* at least, into a form that could inflict no further harm on living humans.

Slowly, cautiously, the kitchen door swung open. It was

one of those that swung both ways on special hinges, for convenience of the café's waitresses, and now a human-looking figure with a long face, curly hair, and dowdy clothes stepped through the opening. Behind the gawky man, two others cleared the threshold, followed by a woman in a long dark dress, her round face white as chalk.

"You'll come with us," the first man through the doorway said.

"I doubt it," Thorn replied, and fired one barrel of the coach gun. Two of the intruders vanished in a cloud of gunsmoke and a substance that resembled dust. The blast made Laurel's ears ring, but she kept her eyes open and saw the other pair of their assailants, man and woman, trying to escape.

Thorn fired again, obliterating both of them. Before the refuse of their swift disintegration settled, Thorn had cracked the shotgun to eject its empty shells from smoking barrels and replaced them with two more extracted from his bandolier.

He turned to Laurel and said, "We have to go. The whole street will have heard those shots."

"Where to?" she asked him.

"I was thinking of the church," he said.

Hezekiah Gates not only heard the shotgun blasts; he *felt* them like two hammer strokes against his skull. He faltered, reeling for an instant, then regained control and clinched his fists, a snarl of fury printed on his face.

Four of his loyal parishioners, victims of Bloody Bill in 1864, were gone for good. He did not clearly understand the manner of their passing, since they were impervious to gunfire, but he knew that they were truly dead this time, the same way he had felt three others die for the last time, not long before. There might be others slain by now, for all he knew, some silent means of killing them, but time had taught him that he did not feel the last, true death of spirits drawn to Lazarus, who had not perished in the Civil War atrocity eleven years ago. Somehow—what did it matter now?—there was a difference between the incomers and those who'd spent their Earthly lives in Lazarus until guerrillas slaughtered them.

One of God's little mysteries, Gates thought, and shrugged it off.

Gates was one of those mysteries, himself, as was the very town he served. Who else in all of mankind's history had been a pastor to the dead—and dead himself, at that? A modest man when he was breathing air, Gates wondered if he were unique in all the world, and why that task was handed down to him. Why was he moved by the Almighty's hand to do the things he did each anniversary in Lazarus, with his parishioners?

Revenge was part of it, he understood. The Good Book laid it down in Jeremiah, Chapter 15: "O Lord, thou knowest: remember me, and visit me, and revenge me of my persecutors; take me not away in thy longsuffering: know that for thy sake I have suffered rebuke." Gates spoke the words aloud as he led members of his flock down Main Street, on the way to Adeline's. He knew the men and women whom they sacrificed each anniversary were not the people who had swept through Lazarus with torches, guns and swords—and yet, shedding their blood appeased Gates and the rest while they slept for another year.

It was not for the minister to understand, much less to judge. He simply did as he was told by the omniscient voice inside his head. When he had sacrificed enough, God would decide and let him know the bill was paid.

Until that day, Gates still had work to do.

Most of the town had rushed toward Adeline's, responding to the shots they'd heard, with Pastor Gates directing them. Suspicion drew Finch Farrell and his little group of half a dozen volunteers off toward the edge of town instead, focusing on the livery.

Instinct told Farrell only one man in their latest company of honored guests might have the wherewithal to stand against the citizens of Lazarus this night, when they were strong and caught up in the yearly ritual that fed them energy from those they sacrificed. It was the odd man out, who'd saved the stagecoach passengers from highway robbery but was not one of them per se: Gideon Thorn.

From the first moment he arrived in Lazarus there was an air of *difference* about him, nothing Farrell could identify by looking at the stranger, but he *felt* it. Thorn had walked strange paths before and managed to survive the journey, pressing on to reach his final destination here—but he would not go down without a fight.

And if he chose to flee, a possibility Farrell could not rule out, Thorn would retrieve his animals.

The marshal thought of Cletus Stokes, one of their incomers, who had appeared in Lazarus on last year's anniversary and fallen into place quite easily as blacksmith for a day. It might take years to learn his story, and the reason why he'd been attracted to the town, instead of moving on when he was dead. Incomers seldom spilled their tales right off. Some who'd arrived in 1865 and '66 still hadn't shared the details of their passing from the Earthly plane.

None of that mattered now. Farrell was focused on the fact that when he had delivered Julius Coffey to the Holy Resurrection Chapel, passing through the swarm of eager faces in the sanctuary, he had not seen Stokes among them. Possibly that was an oversight, or maybe Cletus had been late arriving, though such tardiness was virtually unheard-of.

No, something had happened at the livery, and Farrell meant to find out what that was.

He reached the stable, led his makeshift posse through the open double doors in front—and stopped immediately, feeling Death. Not like the offerings who still awaited their redemption in the church, but rather true death, blotting out a disembodied soul from Lazarus, sweeping that individual beyond recall.

"Stay here," he ordered, and proceeded through the livery alone. He saw at once that Thorn's two animals—the gray stallion and his pack mule—were missing from their stalls. A little further in, he was distracted by an ashen circle on the floor. As he bent closer, Farrell saw it was composed of powder, each grain carrying the scent of brimstone, known to common living men as sulfur.

Farrell might have gasped if he were still a living, breathing man. He *did* recoil from the proximity of true death to a townsman, even though Cletus had been a recent incomer and therefore lowest on the totem pole in Lazarus, when it came down to sharing in the sacrifice. Now, he would never taste that glorious reward—but was he better off than Farrell and the rest, for that?

Thrusting those doubts away from him, the marshal turned upon his followers, all of them staring at the dust of a departed soul around his boots. "Fan out!" he ordered them. "You seek the man in black, Gideon Thorn."

"Has he not fled?" one of the others asked.

"Not yet," said Farrell, though he couldn't have explained his certainty.

"But Finch, his animals—"

"They're gone," Farrell admitted, "but he won't leave any travelers with us if he can help it. Now, *find him!*"

They dispersed, Farrell emerging from the stable on their heels and peering off along Main Street, toward Adeline's where he could see a crowd of townsfolk jostling on the street. Thorn might believe that he could save the other stagecoach passengers, but he was wrong.

This time, the gift of Life would cost him everything.

Heading for the Holy Resurrection Chapel was a risky move. Thorn knew it, understood why Laurel was reluctant—and, in fact, he had no concrete plan of what to do when they arrived. He only knew that other passengers, along with Dempsey Poppert and his shotgun guard, had been delivered to the church for the climactic action of the festival which seemed to be the sole reason for martyred residents of Lazarus appearing on the anniversary of their demise.

What they hoped to do, how they'd decided that the blood of strangers would complete the ritual, Thorn couldn't say. He'd never dealt with ghosts before, had no idea if these were typical of Earthbound spirits as a whole or ghastly deviations from the "norm," condemned to mayhem by their bloody end. And, truth be told, he didn't care.

The anniversary, he now surmised, meant Thorn was

on the clock. He couldn't guess whether the day of sacrifice would end for Lazarus at midnight or with coming of the new dawn on September 26, but he could not afford to wait and see. If he had any hope of rescuing the others, salvaging their lives if not their sanity, he had to *act*.

But how?

A charge into the Holy Resurrection Chapel, blasting with the coach gun, would be suicide. He might drop six or eight, if the townsfolk were clumped together, but the rest would swarm and overpower him before he could reload. A futile gesture, nothing gained except his own demise and Laurel's, if she followed him inside.

What, then?

Huddled beside a dry goods store, hearing the hunt behind them, ranging down the thoroughfare, he eyed the church with its white steeple and a six-foot cross on top. It was the tallest building found in Lazarus, the symbol that surmounted it resembling a lightning rod.

If only it were stormy out, a bolt from the night sky might solve his problem in a flash—or would it fry the hostages, along with the undead inhabitants of Lazarus?

And if he could not trust in Nature to provide relief...

"What's that?" Laurel hissed at him.

Thorn was surprised that he had voiced his thought aloud. "I said, 'I wonder if they have a ladder leading to the roof'."

"What are you thinking?"

"I'm not sure. First thing, I need to find some kerosene or something similar."

Laurel Dycus blinked at Thorn, trying to grasp the plan that he couldn't explain himself, still forming in his mind. She glanced across Main Street and said, "I'd try there, first. The hardware store."

"Good thinking," he replied. "With any luck, I won't be long. You just stay here and—"

"Not a chance in Hell," she cut him off. "I'll stick with you."

"But—"

"No buts," Laurel said. "You may be crazy, but you're all I've got right now."

FIFTEEN

"The hell is goin' on here, Dempsey?" Warren Mapes inquired. He kept his voice pitched low, not quite a whisper, leaning in toward Poppert as he spoke.

"You slept through most of it," the stagecoach driver answered, from the corner of his mouth. "The way it's lookin' now, you mighta been well off to stay asleep."

"They all gone crazy?"

"Beats hell outa me," Poppert confessed. "I come to see you at the doc's place, after sundown, and the friggin' sawbones knocked me out with chloroform. Next thing I know, I wake up here, in church."

Mapes looked around, picked out some of the passengers they'd carried into Lazarus—was it just yesterday? As muddled as he was from drugs he had received, he started counting heads and came up one short when he's been around their little circle twice, noting the ring of hostile faces that surrounded them.

"Somebody's missin'," he told Poppert. "Can't quite put my finger on which one, though."

"It's the governess, that Dycus woman. This bunch missed her somehow. God knows where she is."

"And Thorn, too. Guy that helped us out."

"I noticed that right off," Poppert replied.

"Think they's together?"

"How 'n hell would I know that? I'm stuck here 'cause I tried to help you out."

"Who asked you?" Mapes shot back from force of habit, from their longtime friendly bickering while riding on the stage.

"So, that's what you call gratitude? This is the last damned time I—"

"Silence!" growled a burly man, one of their captors in the chapel. "No one gave you leave to speak."

"Nobody *has* to give us leave," Mapes answered back. "It's still a damn free country, last I heard. You oughta brush up on the Constitution ever now and then, you lummox."

The big man swung a haymaker at Mapes. Instead of flattening the coach guard, though, his meaty fist *passed through* the target's face from left to right, leaving Mapes staggering, still on his feet but awkwardly light-headed, as if somebody had pumped him full of hydrogen, the floating gas, while he had been sedated. Mapes lurched into Poppert, who was quick enough to catch him, while his husky challenger gaped at his fist as if he'd just then noticed it for the first time.

"No substance!" said the big man, sounding shocked.

"We need the pastor and the marshal," said a woman standing at his elbow, scowling at the prisoners.

"They shall return soon, with the others," said another man, making no move to join the weird, one-sided fight.

"The hell is goin' on here?" Mapes repeated his original question.

"Can't answer that," said Poppert. "But we need to get as far away from here as possible. You up to runnin'?"

"Watch me," Mapes replied.

They both broke for the chapel's exit, charging head-on into some of those who held them prisoner, striking to right and left with elbows as they ran. Instead of toppling bodies, though, it felt as though they had collided with wet blankets hanging on a clothesline, furled around them, clinging to them as they struggled toward the door. Mapes saw some of the faces twist and spread, the way he'd seen bystanders look when he was well into his cups and things began to blur. The hands that clutched at him felt rubbery —not weak, so much as insubstantial—but the crowd had numbers on its side and he was dragged down, kicking like a madman, to the floor.

Thorn scanned the thoroughfare before he made his break across it, hearing Laurel's petticoats rustling behind him all the way. He stopped short in the recessed entryway of Abrams' Hardware, hidden by the deeper shadows there, and tried the doorknob without any hope that it would open to his touch.

It was unlocked.

Thorn pushed the door wide-open and went in behind his sawed-off coach gun, index finger on both triggers, with the hammers cocked. When no one rushed him from the darkened room, he started to relax a little, feeling Laurel bump against him where he stood.

"I think they missed us crossing," she said, breathless from their run.

"We can't waste time, regardless," he replied. "Where would you look for kerosene?"

"A backroom, maybe," she suggested. "But I've never run a store."

"As good a place to start as any," Thorn agreed, and wound his way past tools displayed on racks, boxes of nails and other fasteners lined up on shelves in order of their size. They passed around a counter and the entrance to a backroom opened up before them like a cave's mouth, black and menacing.

"Hang back a step or two," Thorn cautioned. "Just in case."

Laurel, clutching the blacksmith's poker, said, "I'm with you all the way."

Clearing the threshold to the storage room, they passed without being attacked once more. Thorn was convinced by now that the proprietors were with their ghastly fellows in the Holy Resurrection Chapel, or else scouring the streets for Thorn and Laurel. Either way, he felt oppressed by passing time and knew that they had none to spare.

Five minutes later, Thorn found what he sought: a shelf of gallon jugs, each labeled KEROSENE. He had no thoughts on what a town composed of ghosts would use it for, why lamps were even needed, wondering if it was simply there to augment the image of a normal working store.

He took one town, screwed off its top, and sniffed the contents, half expecting water in the place of kerosene. Instead, the fumes rushed out at him and brought tears to his eyes.

"It's real," he said. "I'm guessing two gallons should do

the trick, and now I'll need a length of rope, say three feet long."

"What for?" she asked.

"To help me carry it."

Not clear on what he meant, she said, "Rope's over here," and led him to the storeroom's western wall. There, coils of rope hung looped on wooden pegs.

Thorn chose a loop at random, pulled out some four feet of brand-new rope, and cut it with his Bowie knife. That done, he knotted one end of the remnant through the handle of each gallon jug, testing them, then stooped down and slipped the rope over his neck. Rising, he took the weight across his shoulders, grimacing a little as the rope tightened.

"Okay," he said. "Let's go."

"Hold on," said Laurel, barely audible. "I think there's someone in the store."

Finch Farrell didn't see the fugitives cross Main Street, since his back was turned to that end of the thoroughfare. He *sensed* them crossing, though, their raw vitality so far removed from his and totally at odds with Farrell's separation from the realm of daily life that their proximity set off alarms inside his head.

He spun to face the far end of the street, saw nothing he could aim a gun or finger at, but started off in that direction anyway. Each forward step he took increased the feeling that he was upon the right track, homing on the targets he required to make the sacrifice complete. The marshal almost drew his six-gun, then decided that he wouldn't need it for the job at hand.

Granted, Thorn had disposed of Cletus Stokes by method still unknown, and Farrell had experienced the tremors spread by other souls dispatched that night, coincident with gunfire along Main Street, but he couldn't put the two events together in his mind. One great advantage of the dead was being safe from most devices and the various diseases known to kill mankind. There were a few, of course —too few to mention, really—and it worried Farrell to suppose that Thorn was conscious of them.

How could that happen? Why would he know?

Farrell himself could only name three methods: iron, salt, and flame—the latter useless unless it was coupled with archaic rituals of exorcism long forgotten by most priests. Today, men of the cloth claimed ghosts were phantoms of diseased imagination or, perhaps in very rare cases, false apparitions cast up by the Evil One himself. Farrell had never passed the time of day with Lucifer, much less with the Almighty. In fact, he couldn't say with any certainty that either one of them existed, but if it came to choosing one, he'd have to say the anniversaries of Lazarus were more in tune with something conjured from the pit than from on high.

Nearing the stretch of Main Street where he'd felt the runaways, Farrell slowed down and set his mind to work scanning the storefronts. At this hour on an anniversary, he should be able to detect...

Yes! There it was: a pulse of warmth that should not have existed inside Abrams' Hardware Store. A throbbing beat of Life.

Scratch that. *Two* beating hearts, the only ones in Lazarus not penned inside the Holy Resurrection Chapel at that moment. He could track them now, as surely as he could by staring at them in broad daylight, totally exposed.

The only thing that Farrell didn't understand was *why*. What brought them to the hardware store? Not simply to employ it as a hiding place. His mind rejected that at once. They had some other motive, and he guessed Gideon Thorn was at the root of it. The man in black was onto something, or believed he was.

It was Finch Farrell's job to stop him short of finding out.

He reached the wooden sidewalk, stepped up onto it, and found the shop's front door ajar. A gentle touch propelled it inward, swinging easily on hinges that appeared to be well oiled. He didn't understand how Lazarus could rise each year, for just one day, in near-perfect condition, nor did it concern him now.

His quarry was almost within his reach, and they would not escape from him again.

"Hurry! Find them!" Reverend Gates was shouting, when the words caught in his throat and he was staggered by a double shock. He might have lost his balance, falling, if that had been possible, but his excitement and the celebration's swift approach both buoyed him somehow, a feeling he remembered from last year's festivities but had forgotten in his rush to find the sacrificial stragglers.

The ceremony!

There was trouble at the church. Gates knew that much instinctively, without grasping precisely what was wrong. Some kind of turmoil, where there should have been a swelling harmony among the members of his flock, anticipating what would follow when the last of those ordained for sacrifice were captured and returned. What was it that disturbed him so? Resistance by the captives, or had someone from the town itself forgotten his instructions? Were they pushing on without him in their yearly thirst for living blood?

"Wait! Stop!" he snapped at those around him, noting that some of them *shimmered* now, under a gibbous moon, as if the sheer force of his voice caused them to waver momentarily between the physical and insubstantial, trembling on the borderline between Earthly and spiritual planes. A couple of their faces blanked out for a heartbeat, then swam back from somewhere else, jaws slack as if they had been stunned, eyes vacant.

"Get back to the chapel," he commanded, noting their surprised incomprehension. Fumbling for an explanation, Gates fell short and simply barked, "There's trouble at the chapel. Now! Make haste!"

Some did as they were told, rushing away, while others straggled out behind the leaders, glancing back at him, as if he'd lost his senses and was speaking gibberish. It was the first time that he could remember, either living or since he was cut down in his prime, eleven years ago, when anyone —even the town's few unbelievers—looked at him with such pure skepticism.

They could likely feel the rippling shock waves from the Holy Resurrection Chapel for themselves, of course, almost as clearly as he could. They knew something was happening, outside of his control, and now they doubted him because of it. Dissension in the ghostly ranks was absolutely new, unthinkable since Lazarus had risen from the smitten plain for the first time in 1865. They'd only had one guest that year, a hapless wanderer, and there had barely been enough of him to go around, but every appetite was whetted, and the harvest during years to come was more substantial.

This would be the best of all, so far—unless Gates let it slip away from him.

"Make haste, I said!" he bellowed at the stragglers, voice strained when he thought the sheer force of his will should have propelled them toward the church as one. Gates followed them, feeling *depleted* somehow, nearly sapped of strength, forced for a moment to consider each step forward, fighting not to falter and collapse.

He'd reached a level with the hardware store, scene of the premature slaughter on Friday night, when more gunfire rang out and he was staggered by a wave of pain that almost brought him down. One of his best, most loyal parishioners was gone now, passing underneath his feet through solid rock and soil as if hellbound.

Gates nearly stumbled, saved himself at the last instant with an outstretched hand, although his fingertips sank farther than they should into the dry soil of the thoroughfare. Recovering, he pressed on toward the church, lurching as much as running now, desperate to discover what had happened to his flock.

"I feel you," said a man's voice from the shop's main public room. It had a taunting sound. "I smell you hiding there."

Laurel Dycus knew that voice, though she had only heard it briefly, and she was about to speak a name when Thorn reached out and clapped a hand over her mouth. She blinked at him and saw him slowly shake his head, lips puckered as he shushed her.

Marshal Farrell. He had found them somehow. Laurel

could not imagine how he'd done it, but she suddenly felt trapped, sensed that a mad rush through the backdoor of the hardware store would offer no escape in fact. She had no way of knowing if the lawman was alone, but only one set of approaching footsteps was immediately audible.

Gideon Thorn crouched slightly, setting down his yoke of rope and kerosene jugs, straightening again to cock the coach gun he was carrying.

"I heard that," Farrell mocked the sound. "You'd be amazed how sounds and smells take on new strength during the celebration of our anniversary. I'd almost say it was miraculous."

His shadow fell across the storeroom's threshold, then the marshal stepped inside, smiling. He glanced at Thorn's shotgun and said, "You think I'm frightened of your little toy, there? What a fool you are! But still, at least you try."

"I do my best," Thorn said, standing his ground.

"It's understandable that neither of you wants to die," said Farrell. "Do you think *I* did, that night? But I'm the living—well, the *dying*—proof that something lies beyond the pale for all of us. I don't know where the spirits of our sacrifices go, but none has yet returned to Lazarus. We must have sent them on to someplace better, as the pastor says."

"Or else, you just destroyed them," Thorn replied. "Cheated them out of whatever should lie beyond."

Farrell frowned at him for a moment, then resolved his indecision with a headshake. "No. You're wrong, of course. The pastor wouldn't lie."

"What makes you think he knows the truth, when you don't?" Laurel challenged him.

"Quiet, woman! The Good Book says 'let your women be silent in church'."

"Does this look like a church?" she replied, with a sneer.

"Blasphemy! And I've wasted enough time. You're coming with me, whether—"

Thorn fired a blast into Finch Farrell's chest from a range of six feet, give or take. The marshal's image wavered, shivering before their eyes, and then disintegrated from the boots upward. The last thing Laurel saw was his astounded, unbelieving face, before it winked out like the Cheshire cat in Lewis Carroll's story *Alice's Adventures in Wonderland*, published during the war.

And like that, he was gone.

Before it fully registered on Laurel, Thorn had already reloaded and had taken up his heavy yoke again. "Snap out of it," he told her. "We don't have a minute left to spare."

SIXTEEN

Orin Pinkham was borne along Main Street as if floating, the hands beneath him barely there, almost dreamlike, although he had to classify this as a nightmare, possibly continuing the mental shock he'd registered that morning, waking to an empty satchel where his treasure had been hidden when he fell asleep.

Tears streamed down Pinkham's cheeks and he was babbling, not a prayer per se, but mumbled imprecations to the night sky overhead, alive with twinkling stars. Was someone looking down on him right now, amused by how his wasted life was ending? Did the watchers make sport of his plight, or simply shake their heads, bewildered and ashamed on his behalf?

A fragment of his mind wondered exactly what the hell was happening to him, but comprehension had deserted him by now. Jostling along the sidewalk, nearly airborne, Pinkham felt a strange sense of elation, *liberation,* as if all requirements for a rational decision and a course of action had been stripped from him. He sensed that nothing more would be required of him, except perhaps for one last act to finish off the bleak pastiche of life, and it surprised the banker that he was not more afraid.

But when he thought about it, what more did he have to lose?

The church was closer now, its twin doors standing open, and lamplight spilling out onto the thoroughfare. Pinkham lifted his head to catch a glimpse inside, then gave it up as too exhausting, thankful that he did not have to walk the final steps before he laid his burden down. Townsfolk were doing all the work for him, and he was grateful for their generosity.

Three wooden steps led up into the chapel. Some of Pinkham's bearers stumbled on them, but there were enough with steady feet and grips to keep his slack form hoisted overhead. It struck him that the church smelled strange, a burning odor, but he guessed it must be lamps and candles lighted to illuminate its chapel for the ceremony. What did he know, anyway, when he had set foot in a church no more than half a dozen times in twenty years?

Speaking of feet, the people—*were* they people?—who had carried Pinkham now set him on his and held him steady till he had regained his balance. Counting heads, he spotted four former companions from the stagecoach, plus both members of its crew. Which one was missing? Ah, the governess, probably hiding somewhere if she had been quick enough, and their young savior from the holdup, Mr. Thorn. He seemed resourceful, but in Pinkham's present state, he doubted whether either of them would escape.

As for himself, after his fleeting struggle on the street, Pinkham had felt no great urge to escape whatever might befall him next. He had arrived at what he took to be his final destination, and it seemed to be that he belonged precisely where he was.

Whatever happened next, Pinkham supposed that he would get what he deserved.

Behind him, with a sound like rushing wind, the minister and more of his peculiar worshipers entered the church. The pastor's eyes were fairly glowing, hands raised overhead to still the babbling all around him now, as he addressed his flock.

"Move toward the altar," he commanded. "Bring the travelers we have. Our time is growing short."

Thorn stood in shadow, Laurel at his side, and watched the last few stragglers make their way inside the Holy Resurrection Chapel, tall doors closing after them. It pleased him that they left no guards stationed outside the church, to watch Main Street, and with no windows facing on the thoroughfare, he thought they should be safe from watchers, at least momentarily.

"Let's do it," he told Laurel, and stepped down from the sidewalk, jogging toward the church. Its bell began tolling again, but when no one appeared outside, he guessed that it was not alerting celebrants to his approach.

Behind him, Laurel had the shotgun now and wore the bandolier of extra rounds, having convinced him that she knew enough about the weapon's handling, even if she'd never shot a man—or ghost—with a twelve-gauge before. Thorn trusted her enough to let the coach gun go. Besides, if he could find a way to scale the church's steeple, he was bound to need both hands.

Upon arrival at the church, loud voices audible inside—could it be possible that they were singing "Onward Christian Soldiers"?—Thorn and Laurel ducked around the south side of the church. His worries about climbing to the steeple's pinnacle were instantly assuaged, as Thorn beheld a ladder, or rather a series of ladders, nailed to the side of the church, painted white like the rest of the building. The first would take him from ground level to the sloping roof. The next, fixed to the roof itself, would place him at the south side of the steeple. There, a final ladder granted access to the belfry and the cross on top of it, presumably for purposes of outside maintenance, while any work on bells, bell ropes and such would be performed inside.

His route was clear. Now, all he had to do was make that climb without dropping his hard-won jugs of kerosene or plummeting to break his neck, spine, arms and legs. Once he had reached the pinnacle and carried out his master plan, Thorn would be forced to climb back down again—this time while flames consumed the Holy Resurrection Chapel from above.

Simple in theory. As to carrying it off...

"Remember," he told Laurel, as he stood with one foot on a ladder rung, hands wrapped around another, higher up, "if anyone shows up, do what you can to keep them off my back. But if it looks like you could be surrounded, run like hell and save yourself."

"Hell's where we are right now," she told him, with a crooked little smile. "Where would I go?"

Thorn couldn't answer that. Instead, he told her, "I don't know what to expect when it's lit up. The others, already inside..."

"Will have to take their chances," Laurel finished for him. "Anyway, you're giving them a chance. They've got none, as it is."

Inside the church, the singing stopped. A booming voice was raised, telling the congregants, "Bring forth the female sinner! Let her lead the way!" Immediately after that, Thorn's ears rang with a woman's doomed, god-awful scream of fear, mingled with pain.

"That's Mrs. Mottinger," said Laurel. "Hurry, now!"

Thorn pushed off with his right foot and began to climb.

After calming his parishioners, Reverend Gates mounted the dais, raised his hands, and led them in three rousing hymns. The first was "Battle Hymn of the Republic," followed by "My Hope is Built"—best known for its refrain: "On Christ the solid rock I stand"—and finally the ringing strains of "Onward Christian Soldiers," closing out the musical component of their festival.

In truth, Gates couldn't say with any certainty that he or any of his spectral followers still qualified as Christians, or that they were standing on the so-called solid rock. If all he had been taught from childhood and had later taught to others was the "gospel truth," Gates thought they should have woken up in heaven after they were massacred by heathen traitors to the Union on this date, eleven years ago. Instead, it seemed that they were doomed, or cursed, to reenact a measure of that slaughter every year, their violence toward living strangers gaining...what, for those responsible?

Despite his own deep-seated doubts, Gates went ahead each year, each anniversary, because he was convinced he had no choice. If God or Someone Else had brought him and the other citizens of Lazarus back to a vague semblance of life on this, their special day, who was he to refuse?

The last hymn ended on a rising note—*With the cross of*

Jesus going on before—then ringing silence settled over those inside the Holy Resurrection Chapel for a moment, until Gates cried out to them once more.

"Bring forth the female sinner! Let her lead the way!"

His followers greeted the call with cheers, manhandling Florence Mottinger as they conveyed her toward the pulpit. Straining to escape and reach her helpless husband, gripped by two men with the strength of ten, she cried out, "Eldridge, help!" His streaming tears and lunging, easily restrained, were symbols of his impotence.

Gates reached inside his cassock to remove the carving knife he carried there, its twelve-inch blade tucked underneath his belt. He raised it overhead, shouting, "I strike the first blow to begin our festival and once again to fertilize this consecrated ground with blood until the Day of Judgment finally arrives!"

A cheer went up from every throat inside the church, except for the awestruck and cringing prisoners. As usual, they did not seem to recognize the vital role they played in satisfactory completion of the sacred ritual. Not that it mattered to the end result. There was no rule Gates knew of that the sacrificial subjects should be willing volunteers.

In fact, he was convinced, their terror added something to the ceremony, bringing members of his congregation more *alive* before their time ran out again at midnight, as it always did.

Gates watched his people lift the woman off her feet and stretch her out upon a table to his right, draped in white linen for its service as an altar. While she struggled, writhing like a serpent penned with a forked stick, Flo Mottinger began to curse her captors, using language that no Christian lady ought to know or understand, much less allow to foul her tongue or reach the ears of others in a House of God.

Gates moved to stand above her, wedged one hand beneath her jaw to close her mouth without a risk of being bitten, and advised his congregants, "The time has come! We strike tonight for honor and in strict obedience to Deuteronomy, chapter thirty-two, verse forty-two: 'I will make mine arrows drunk with blood, and my sword shall devour flesh; and that with the blood of the slain and of the captives, from the beginning of revenges upon the enemy.' Amen!"

The chapel echoed with "amens" from every throat except those of the prisoners. When they were stilled, Gates roared, drew back his knife, and plunged it deep into the wriggling woman's chest.

Laurel Dycus has deceived Gideon Thorn. In fact, she *had* shot someone with a double-barreled twelve-gauge once before, but only in the leg, which had to be removed. The man on the receiving end of that blast had been raving drunk, maniacal, racing around a brothel she administered in Hopkinsville, Kentucky, slashing at the girls with a straight razor. Laurel had warned him half a dozen times before she took him down, and while the Christian County sheriff filed no charges, he'd encouraged her to find another town without delay.

She watched Thorn climb up to the chapel's roof, encumbered by the swinging jugs secured by rope around his neck, then watched him scramble to the next ladder in turn, the steeple ladder, with his boot soles slipping just enough on shingles underfoot to make her gasp and hold her breath.

Once he was heaving up the final flight of rungs, she left him to it, pivoting to scan Main Street and verify that no one had emerged yet from the Holy Resurrection Chapel's nearby doors.

So far, so good.

The screams from Florence Mottinger had chilled her to the bone, but they had ended swiftly, telling Laurel that the woman had been killed somehow. She didn't want to know the details, much less witness them, and she was not about to risk a peek inside the church. Only Gideon Thorn and pure dumb luck had saved her from the same fate as her former fellow traveler. Before she fell into the rabid congregation's hands, Laurel would send a few of them to Hell, then end her own life with at least a modicum of dignity.

More shouting issued from inside the church, their so-called minister exhorting his pathetic, undead sheep to wreak more havoc on their prisoners. Without discerning words, she could not tell if they were marked for murder one by one, or if a savage melee would come next, with all hands joining in the deadly celebration. Laurel would have liked to plug her ears as more screams reached them—all men's voices now, with cheering from the audience participants—but she kept both hands on the shotgun, dual hammers back, her index finger curled inside the trigger guard.

If danger came—make that *when* danger came—Laurel Dycus vowed that she would be prepared. She only hoped that Thorn could do his job and make it down to stand beside her when their final moment came. If they managed to survive it by some miracle, so be it. And if not, at least she'd have the privilege of dying with a man she'd come to think of as a friend.

Halfway through his climb to reach the steeple's crowning decoration, Thorn could feel his arms and shoulders quaking from the strain of two glass gallon jugs tethered around his neck, the rope straining his trapezius muscles and chafing the nape of his neck. He couldn't spare a hand to ease the pressure for a moment, and was worried that a shift of any kind might send the makeshift halter plummeting to brain Laurel Dycus, down below, or shatter on the ground nearby and drench her skirt in wasted kerosene.

He needed every stolen drop of it to carry out his plan—and even then, he had no guarantee of ultimate success.

He was within three yards or so of the open belfry, conscious of the shouts and screams that rose to meet him from inside the church. It sounded like a massacre in progress, and Thorn closed his mind to grim, unbidden images of stagecoach passengers and crew he'd met the day before, suffering torments of the damned from those who actually were. He knew it would have been a suicidal fool's ploy to invade the sanctuary on a rescue mission, two salt rounds against the mob of congregants before they overwhelmed both him and Laurel Dycus, if she'd been deranged enough to follow him inside. Why sacrifice themselves, as well, when Thorn's scheme had at least a chance of working out?

The ghost of a chance, he thought then, and swallowed a note of hysterical laughter before it escaped from his throat.

Thorn reached the open belfry, grasped its sill with one hand, then the other, while his feet braced on the ladder's final, topmost rung. From there, if he was very cautious and kept one hand on the sill, watching his step, he could proceed around the belfry's other sides, depositing his kerosene on three of four while leaving an escape path down the ladder he'd ascended, once a match was struck.

But first, he had to open one of the two jugs.

They both had metal screw caps, better for preventing spillage than the corks employed on many jugs containing other liquids. Thorn loosened the cap of the jug on his left side but left it in place as he started his slow walk around the belfry, placing each step cautiously until he'd reached the side directly opposite the ladder he'd ascended. There, he freed the screw cap, tossed it into darkness somewhere down below, and began the awkward task of wetting down the church's roof without spilling the kerosene over his boots and trouser cuffs.

It took some time, and he considered pouring some directly down the open belfry, but he didn't want its smell or pattering of liquid as it fell inside alerting any of his enemies inside the sanctuary. They would know what he had done once Thorn lit up their chapel of the damned and made his getaway.

Or, if his luck failed, when he died in the attempt.

SEVENTEEN

Julius Coffey was convinced that he had lost his mind. Perhaps one of the rattlesnakes he'd found in his room the first time had struck him, filling his veins with poison, and the venom finally had reached his fevered brain. How else could he explain the wild, atrocious scene inside the Holy Resurrection Chapel which his eyes convinced him he was witnessing?

It made no sense if he was sane, this bacchanalia of violence inside a church, of all places, with townspeople attacking, butchering his fellow stagecoach passengers, the driver and his shotgun guard, while their purported minister loomed over all, his hands like talons clutching at the pulpit, while he shouted exhortations to the mob for even greater excesses, more blood, more suffering.

Madness, he thought. Dear God, please let me be insane!

His life was not supposed to end this way. Coffey had been elected to the legislature, was convinced that he could make his mark there, pass on when he'd served a term or two to higher office, either in the Sunflower State or in the nation's capital. His future was unlimited, the prize was his to grasp—but now, it seemed his only destination would be permanent confinement at a state asylum. And if he was finally released, someday, what sort of future could he count on? Sweeping sidewalks, possibly, or clearing road apples out of the streets in some pathetic prairie town.

All gone, but even being wrapped up in a straitjacket was better than the grisly fantasy being played out before his eyes. The citizens of Lazarus were butchering his fellow travelers, not only hacking, stabbing, rending them, but now reaching *inside* them and cavorting with their innards while he watched, aghast.

The first to die, the thing that had been Florence Mottinger, was now unrecognizable. Her husband had been next, struggling to reach her until three men bore him to the ground and went to work on him with knives. The stagecoach driver and his sidekick fought as best they could against the overwhelming odds, but fell as slashing blades opened their flesh, spilled crimson from their veins. Delbert Akins and the shifty-looking banker, Orin Pinkham, tried to flee but never reached the chapel's exit, swarmed and dragged down while they screamed, torn limb from limb by thrusting, hacking knives.

At last, Julius Coffey stood alone. The mob's blood-smeared participants all turned to him as one, their eyes alight as if from lanterns burning in their skulls. Their smiles were hideous as they advanced on him, clown faces etched in gore, with shreds of cloth and flesh stuck in between their teeth. After a moment, Coffey thought he heard them muttering in unison. He took a moment to decide that they were chanting "Vengeance!" as they closed around him, groping at him, any hope for his retreat cut off.

This isn't happening, he told himself. It's a hallucination.

When the doctors come for me, I'll be sedated. All of this will fade like any other nightmare when I wake.

The first blade slid between his ribs then, scraping bone before it pierced a lung, and Julius Coffey screamed.

Thorn finished emptying his second jug of kerosene around the belfry, screwed its cap back on, then shrugged his harness off and let it fall away from him, the empty glass jugs bouncing once apiece before they arced out into darkness, plunging to the ground below. Immediate relief flooded Thorn's aching neck and shoulders, but he had no time to waste enjoying the sensation.

From the screams that rose to meet him, from the chapel, he knew that a massacre was underway. He might already be too late to stop it, rescue any of the victims from the stagecoach who'd been dragged inside the Holy Resurrection Chapel, but he *could* attempt to end the gruesome festival—and, with a bit of luck, ensure that it did not happen again.

Was fire sufficient to eradicate the curse from Lazarus? Or would his gesture be a hollow, pointless one?

Only one way to know, he thought, and struck a match, applied it to the base of the tall cross atop the Belfry, which he'd also splashed with kerosene, and saw it instantly burst into flame. Recoiling from the sudden heat, Thorn nearly lost his footing, but hung on and started to descend the ladder that had brought him to his present height above the haunted town. Before he'd gone six feet, the sharply sloping roof around the open belfry was on fire, sending smoke signals into darkness overhead, firelight casting the chapel's shadow down the middle of Main Street.

Laurel would see the edifice in flames and would be smart enough to back away from it before it started to collapse. Inside, it seemed to Thorn the screaming had abated for the moment. He imagined the demented shades of Lazarus all staring upward at the belfry, terrified and baffled by the fire, and hoped that all of them would be consumed.

As for the hostages, most likely slaughtered now, perhaps Thorn's act would spare them from revisiting the world they'd known as predators, performing in an endless puppet show which had no meaning for them, but which they could not escape.

If only he could find a way to burn the rest of Lazarus...

When he was halfway down the ladder, hurrying, a swarm of golden sparks blew past Thorn's face. He turned, charting their path, and saw them settle on a nearby rooftop, catching light on shingles that were dry as kindling. Three more rungs toward touchdown, and he saw the nearby roof burst into churning flame.

"Go on, then! Spread!" he called out to the fire, and swallowed down an urge to laugh.

Laurel Dycus saw the Holy Resurrection Chapel burning from the top down, spire surmounted by a six-foot blazing cross, its image seeming five six times that size, as it reflected on the thoroughfare.

Thorn was descending, doing fine so far, and Laurel kept her coach gun pointed at the church's tall twin doors. She had nearly abandoned hope of any other captives getting out alive, and now her first priority was making sure the ghosts of Lazarus did not escape, until they'd been reduced to dust or ash.

Whether that solved the problem for all time or only pushed it back another year, Laurel could not have said and wasn't sure she even cared. By that time she'd be far away from Lazarus and doing everything within her power to erase its memories. If that meant drinking or a spin around the park with laudanum, so be it. She *would not* allow the waking nightmare of the past thirty-six hours to dominate her life in years to come.

She saw sparks drifting from the steeple to the roofs of nearby buildings, settling there, and lighting small fires of their own that swiftly grew and spread. So much the better, to eradicate the stain of Lazarus entirely, if such cleansing was a possibility. With no more mortal residents in town, aside from her and Thorn, a total purge was best. She only hoped that it would do the job, without requiring any further steps or rituals.

As if in answer to her thoughts, a shrill cry wafted from the far end of Main Street, rising out of darkness, echoed by another and another as it drifted on a breeze driven by fire. She turned in that direction, swiveling the coach gun to cover the empty thoroughfare, and squinted to adapt her vision with the firelight blazing up behind her, limiting her range of sight.

Now there were hoofbeats mingled with the sounds of upraised voices, drawing closer, and she leaned in that direction, desperate to see what was approaching from the southern end of Lazarus. She thought of horses bursting from the livery, their stagecoach team, but then remembered that the stable was behind her, farther north, and could not be responsible for the unearthly sounds she heard.

Then what?

Laurel stood her ground, the shotgun's stock clutched underneath her right arm, tight against her ribs, and waited to find out what Lazarus would send against her next.

Thorn's feet touched solid ground and he lurched backward, almost stumbling, as he peered up at the burning Holy Resurrection Chapel looming over him. The sound of raging flames had overshadowed screaming from inside the church, smothering voices with its roar. His heart sank, giving up on those he'd met, however briefly, in the past two days, as heat drove him still farther backward from the church.

"Gideon?" Laurel's voice reached him now, a sense of urgency apparent. "Gideon!"

"I'm here," he said, off-handedly, and turned to find her, but she was not facing him. Instead, her eyes were riveted on Main Street, staring southward, where Thorn's ears now picked out warbling voices and the sound of charging horses, yet unseen.

He rushed to Laurel's side, relieved her of the coach gun and the bandolier of extra salt rounds, wondering what Lazarus, the very mouth of Hell, was going to spit at them next. Thorn knew he hadn't overlooked a group of spectral townspeople, much less a herd of phantom horses, yet the sounds were unmistakable, almost as if...

"Come on!" he snapped at Laurel, clutching her right arm and dragging her away, into a shadowed gap between the blazing church and shops beginning to catch fire along the east side of the thoroughfare. They were still visible, but less so than if they remained outside the Holy Resurrection Chapel with the fire behind them, casting their long shadows down Main Street.

"Who is it?" Laurel asked. "*What* is it?"

"I don't know," he replied, "unless—"

The first riders charged into view, and Thorn's breath caught in his throat. They were gaunt men, bearded, clad in tattered, bloodied uniforms of gray or tan denoting the defunct Confederacy, mounted upon rangy animals that seemed more skin and bones than flesh and muscle. Men and mounts alike were *faded* in appearance, more opaque than solid in the firelight as they galloped headlong toward the flaming outline of the Holy Resurrection Chapel dead ahead.

"That's Bloody Bill!" Thorn blurted out, spotting the leader of the cavalry detachment from a photograph he'd seen in one of Boston's newspapers after the Rebel bandit leader had been killed in 1864. The riders trailing him were obviously dead, as well, but still intent on the fulfillment of a mission they'd completed years ago, during the war, when they were still alive and earning grisly reputations for themselves in Bleeding Kansas.

"But I thought he was dead," said Laurel.

"You were right," Thorn answered. "Which won't stop him raising hell in Lazarus tonight." Gripping her arm, he drew her deeper into midnight shadows, offering a supplication to the pantheon of gods that they would not be seen.

Reverend Hezekiah Gates could feel the flames enveloping his church and congregation, but he did not fear them. As the fire had claimed him once, only to let him rise again, why should the same thing not occur this time? He wished the townsfolk he saw weeping, thrashing, tearing at their pale skin while it blistered, would relax into acceptance of their fate, prepared to rise again on their next anniversary and pick up where they had left off.

What worried Gates, driving a spike of cold fear through his withered heart, was the unearthly howling from outside, accompanied by neighing horses in considerable numbers. He remembered those sounds well enough, and always would. Striding through flames to reach the Holy Resurrection Chapel's double doors, he scowled at the unprecedented two-time interruption of his flock's most sacred ritual.

First, the escapees had set fire to Gates's church, not only slipping through his hands but prematurely ending any celebration of the town's grim anniversary.

And now, it seemed, the very men responsible for so much tragedy in Lazarus were back for more, like uninvited guests intruding on a party and disrupting the festivities with malice in their hearts. Gates seethed at the idea, reached out to grab a burning pew as he passed by and splintered it, turning a portion of the bench into an odd-shaped bludgeon as he neared the chapel doors.

Last time, he'd been consumed by flame while doing nothing, praying for relief to what he now believed to be an apathetic God, disinterested in the trials and suffering of His creations down below, who offered nothing in response to ardent pleas for aid. This time, Gates meant to fight with every ounce of strength that he possessed, and if he failed, at least he would not be remembered as an idiot who took it lying down, mewling and whimpering for help from the beyond.

He burst out through the double doors and found the

Rebel cavalry slowing—a trot now, rather than a gallop—as they closed in on the church. He recognized the leader from their first encounter, wild locks blowing in the night breeze, whiskers tangled like a bird's nest. Bloody Bill was brandishing a six-gun, one of half a dozen that he carried into battle, but his face registered stark surprise.

"I kilt you once!" he shouted out to Gates.

"I recollect it," Gates replied. "How would you like to try again?"

"What is this place?" asked Anderson.

"Your graveyard, Rebel scum!" the minister roared back.

"We'll damn well see about that!" Bloody Bill replied, then spurred his gaunt horse to a gallop, calling out to those behind him, "Charge! No prisoners! No quarter!"

Gates did not retreat. Instead, his clothes and flesh aflame, he ran to meet the leader's loping animal and sprang aboard it, discarding his makeshift club as he wrapped burning arms around Bloody Bill's torso and howled with the rest of them, raising his voice to the stars overhead.

Anderson's ghostly mount charged up the chapel steps and through the flaming mouth of its entrance, other guerrillas falling into line without a second thought, whooping and yipping like a pack of wild dogs as they charged headlong into the raging fire.

Gideon Thorn and Laurel Dycus watched the Rebel cavalry race past them, up the burning wooden steps of Holy Resurrection Chapel, disappearing two-by-two inside the church. It seemed impossible that all of them could fit inside, horses and men alike, but it almost appeared to

Thorn as if each rider passing through the door *dissolved* somehow, consumed before he and his animal had any chance to trample those already trapped inside. It was like watching waste paper tossed into an incinerator, blackened to a crisp and swept straight up the chimney—or, in this case, out the belfry—in a flash.

A crackling sound, far overhead, warned Gideon of danger in the offing, and he pulled Laurel even farther back, just as the blackened, smoking cross detached itself from its exalted place on high, and plummeted to earth, exploding into shards of charcoal as it struck the ground. Thorn half-imagined that he felt a tremor rumble through the ground beneath his feet, and turned to see the rest of Lazarus in flamed, rooftops collapsing as the walls supporting them burned through and fell apart.

"Is this the end of it?" Laurel asked him, shouting to be heard above the roaring fire.

Gideon shrugged, answered, "I don't know. This is all brand-new to me."

"I hope it's over," Laurel said. "I'd *pray* it was, but God and I haven't been on the best of terms, for twenty years or so."

"If He exists," Thorn said, raising a hand to touch the silver pendants that he wore around his neck, "I doubt that He had any part of what happened in Lazarus tonight."

"What do we do now?" she inquired.

"Try not to get ourselves burned to a crisp before the fires die down. At least we won't be cold out here, tonight."

"You plan on *sleeping* here?"

"I need to fetch my animals from where I left them, north of town," he said. "You should be safe enough if you wait here without me, or—"

"Forget that. I'd no more stay here in Lazarus alone than I'd sleep with a grizzly in his winter den."

"Okay. We have a hike ahead of us. The firelight ought to help with part of it, at least."

"I miss the city," she declared, as they began to walk northward. "Small towns have never worked out well for me."

"Not much call for a governess, I guess," he said, feeling a little smile begin.

She caught him at it, snorted, and replied, "I guess that must be it."

EPILOGUE

When dawn broke over Lazarus, Thorn saw that fire had spared the livery, its frame just scorched around the edges, otherwise intact. It was a nice surprise to find the four strong horses from the stagecoach team unharmed, although it took a goodly while to calm them down after the night's calamity of flames, smoke, and an atmosphere of chaos that began to dissipate as gray light turned into rose, and then to warming day.

"We're lucky," Laurel said. "I figured I'd be riding on your mule until we hit another town."

"Bell has a full load as it is," Thorn said, omitting what the animal had thought of carrying a female human off for miles across the Kansas prairie. "Now you can have your pick. Saddles and tack are still hanging inside the stable. Ride whichever one you like and sell the rest to get a stake, wherever you end up."

"Wherever *I* end up?" She lost a little color from her cheeks. "You're leaving me alone?"

"You should be fine," he said. "Less than a day's ride due

north to find another settlement, and this one's on the map. No guesswork about whether people in it are alive or not."

"And you?"

"I'm heading west from here, toward Colorado. Other work to do."

"Mind if I ask what kind?"

"I doubt that you'd believe me."

"After *this?* Christ, that must be some story."

"I won't know until I get there," Thorn replied, "and have a look around. Come on. I'll help you saddle up and get all squared away."

"What do I tell the law in the next town?"

"You've got some hours to decide. If I were you, I'd stay away from ghosts and keep it simple. Say the town caught fire, you don't know how, and went up like a tinder box. You made it out. The others didn't. You should leave out Bloody Bill."

"And what if no one knows that Lazarus ... came back?"

"Don't give the town a name. Just talk about the stage, how it got stopped and all, then jump straight to the fire. If someone wants to check your story, they can see the ashes for themselves."

"I guess. You know, I just wish..."

"What."

She shook her head. "Forget it. Let's go see about that ride. We're burning daylight."

Nodding, Thorn walked with her to the stable, feeling saddened in a way that he could not define. But Breckenridge was waiting for him, and beyond it, other mysteries as yet untold. Before the sun went down again, he would be well away from Lazarus, its ghosts, and any taint that might still linger in its soil.

And if he ever thought about returning some September, just to see what happened next, he hoped his willpower would take him down some other road and lead him safely home.

A LOOK AT: MOUNTAIN DEVILS (GIDEON THORN 4)

BY MICHAEL NEWTON

From deep in the forest comes a howl... and the hunt begins.

Gideon Thorn's search for the thing that destroyed his family leads him to California's deep forests, where loggers are being torn apart by something primal.

Suspicions center on the Omah—part legend, part monster.

Thorn joins an expedition of opportunists, scientists, and showmen to track the beast. But as clues mount—strategic attacks, eerie wood-knocks, even telepathic contact—it becomes clear: the Omah are real. And they're fighting back.

As the body count rises, Thorn must choose sides in a war between greed and nature—while the mystery of his past still waits in the shadows.

AVAILABLE DECEMBER 2025

ABOUT THE AUTHOR

A California native, Michael Newton published over 215 books under his own name and various pseudonyms since 1977. He began writing professionally as a "ghost" for author Don Pendleton on the best-selling Executioner series. With 104 episodes published to date, Newton nearly tripled the number of Mack Bolan novels completed by creator Pendleton himself.